Betsy *and the* Emperor

Staton Rabin

Simon Pulse
New York * London * Toronto * Sydney

SIMON PULSE

An imprint of Simon & Schuster Children's Publishing Division
1230 Avenue of the Americas, New York, NY 10020
Text copyright © 2004 by Staton Rabin
All rights reserved, including the right of reproduction
in whole or in part in any form.
SIMON PULSE and colophon are registered
trademarks of Simon & Schuster, Inc.
Also available in a Margaret K. McElderry Books hardcover edition.
Designed by Jessica Sonkin
The text of this book was set in Filosophia.
Manufactured in the United States of America
First Simon Pulse edition April 2006
2 4 6 8 10 9 7 5 3
The Library of Congress has cataloged the hardcover edition as follows:
Rabin, Staton.
Betsy and the emperor / Staton Rabin.—1st ed.
p. cm.
Summary: In 1815 on the remote island of Saint Helena, fourteen-year-old
Betsy Balcombe develops a friendship with Napoleon Bonaparte who, after his
defeat at Waterloo, is brought there as an exile and is housed with her family.
ISBN-13: 978-0-689-85880-2 (hc.)
ISBN-10: 0-689-85880-9 (hc.)
1. Napoleon I, Emperor of the French, 1769–1821—Juvenile fiction.
2. Abell, Lucia Elizabeth Balcombe, d. 1871—Juvenile Fiction.
[1. Napoleon I, Emperor of the French, 1769–1821—Fiction.
2. Abell, Lucia Elizabeth Balcombe, d. 1871—Fiction. 3. Friendship—Fiction.
4. Saint Helena—History—19th century—Fiction.] I. Title.
PZ7.R1084Be 2004
[Fic]—dc22
2003017628
ISBN-13: 978-1-4169-1336-8 (pbk.)
ISBN-10: 1-4169-1336-X (pbk.)

Acknowledgments

For Anne Lambert and Tom Welch, Dan and Joan Cameron, Sam Donta, Robert Buck, and Doreen Chen and her talented staff (Elizabeth, David, Jarry, and Susan)—who helped me to fly.

With thanks to my agents, Lynn Pleshette and Donna Bagdasarian; film producer Fonda Snyder; and my wonderful and gentle editor, Emma Dryden, whose discernment and good instincts are invaluable to me.

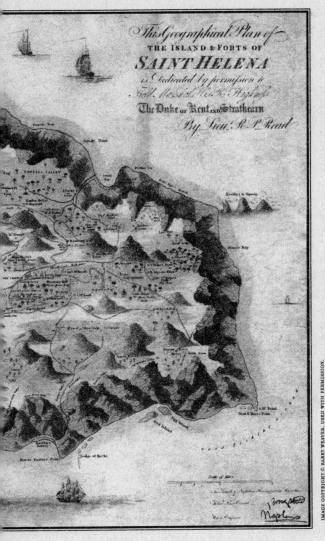

This Geographical Plan of the Island & Forts of Saint Helena
by R. P. Read, London, 1817.

Napoleon Bonaparte

❧

*"I should trouble little about myself
if only I could be sure that someday
our humiliations would be proclaimed
to the world so that those responsible
for them would be covered in shame."*

—NAPOLEON BONAPARTE ON ISLAND OF ST. HELENA

MRS. ABELL.

Betsy Balcombe as an adult

Chapter 1

I opened my bedroom window and inhaled—deeply, joyfully. That familiar, intoxicating odor: night on St. Helena. The sickly-sweet smell of guava and roses hung in the air like ether, just as I'd remembered it. Who would have thought I'd be so glad to return to the place my father and his navy comrades called "Hell in the South Atlantic"?

It was the autumn of 1815. I had been home again at the Briars just three days, from Hawthorne Boarding School in London. I'd shocked my parents by not misbehaving once since my return to St. Helena. Perhaps they believed the knuckle-rapping, head-thumping headmistress of Hawthorne had finally knocked some sense into their younger daughter. I began to wonder it myself. *Blast!* Had I lost my sense of adventure? Would I go soft and ladylike and marry some vain, boot-polished officer of the Fifty-fourth Regiment or His Majesty's Navy—as my sister Jane hoped to do?

Just then two booms of the cannon from the port at Jamestown—the signal for a ship's arrival—broke the stillness. And I knew I remained the Betsy Balcombe of yore. Older, yes. Wiser, perhaps. But never, never willing to settle for a life that's "Tedious-as-Hell in the South Atlantic"!

I threw on my bed jacket and grabbed hold of my ladder—the vine that had, over the years, crept bravely up the red brick walls of the Briars and to the very edge of my windowsill. It was many a night that the vine had been my ladder to adventure. Thank heaven Toby hadn't trimmed it back during my long absence!

I slipped a little as I climbed out the window, and Jane woke with a start. She gave a quiet, girlish scream. I looked over at her, and she was sitting up in her white lacy canopy bed, the covers pulled tight under her chin. I had one leg out the window. My sister glared at me, stern as the headmistress of Hawthorne.

"I'll tell . . . ," Jane threatened coolly.

"Still the little tattler," I said, shaking my head.

Jane was sixteen—two years older than I; old enough to keep secrets.

"You're going into Jamestown, aren't you?"

"Go back to sleep, Jane. If you don't, you'll make your eyes all puffy and you'll turn ugly so none of the young officers will want to marry you."

"Betsy!"

"Good night, Jane."

It was too late for her to stop me. I was already out the window and halfway down the vine. Jane would never think of spoiling her pretty hands by attempting to climb down after me.

I jumped the last few feet to the ground. Then I peered around the corner of the Briars to see who was about. Most of our slaves had already returned to their cabins for the night. Most of the soldiers had turned in too, though there seemed to be a few more sentries on watch than usual.

I rounded the corner of the Briars and dashed to the moon-shaded side of the Pavilion veranda. Suddenly, I heard footsteps in the dank leaves nearby. I froze, listening, trying to quiet my winded breathing so it wouldn't betray me.

"Is me. Only me, missy."

Toby! I'd forgotten the old man liked to stroll by night in the gardens he tended by day. He liked

3

to drink a bit of the island rum too. Not enough to get drunk, though. I breathed a sigh of relief.

"You go for the walk at night—like old time, missy, yes?"

"Yes." I still couldn't see him, but I smelled the rum on his breath. I knew he'd be smiling broadly at me with those remarkably white teeth I used to think were a string of pearls from the seas off his native Haiti.

"Miss Jane with you?"

I laughed. "What do you think?"

"Didn't think yes, missy," he said, chuckling softly. "Didn't think yes."

Toby had been with my family for years and had seen Jane and me grow up. But I knew I was his favorite—even more than the boys.

After a moment he whispered hoarsely: "Ship is here, in Jamestown. Do you know?"

"I heard the signal."

Toby fell silent. Then he sighed and whispered seriously: "All will be very different, St. Helena now. Everything soon change, missy, yes?"

I didn't know what Toby meant. He often said things that sounded mysterious. I knew the island slaves to be very superstitious, so I never took much notice.

"Your papa ask me to cut vines all over," he said with a chuckle. "I leave the one outside missy's window for you coming home."

So Toby knew how I'd escaped from my room at night, and he'd kept my secret! I'd always felt he was one of the few people who understood me.

"Thank you, Toby!"

"Hush!" he whispered. "You wake family all, no Jamestown, no ship to see for missy."

"Good night, Toby," I whispered back, and ran toward Jamestown.

Chapter 2

The warm trade winds of St. Helena gently caressed my legs as I ran—the silent greeting of my old friend, the night. My nightgown rippled, billowed in front of me, filled with the breeze like a great white mainsail. The wind picked up speed, whistling over the jagged edges of the dark, towering mountains all around me. They stood, lined up rocky shoulder to rocky shoulder in their gray, impenetrable armor like ancient warriors, spears of granite piercing the night sky. St. Helena's mountains overwhelmed, even terrified, her visitors: "The Rock," "The Fortress," even "Hell" or "Purgatory" were names by which the island had come to be known. Even residents of St. Helena had no kinder names for her.

I confess I did not like the mountains by day, much less by night. At times they seemed to lean inward, threatening to crush any poor human insect who dared to pass below. Tonight was such a night. And yet, as I ran over the gently sloping valleys—the grazing pastures of the island's small herds of sheep and cows—I felt safe. The grassy hills were a great green cove, a haven where the rocky warriors could not pass. Confidently, I sailed on.

Freedom! It had been so long since I'd tasted its sweetness. Hawthorne had been more of a prison than a boarding school for girls: sundown curfews, grease-laden suppers I would gladly have swapped for the murderer's "bread and water," and sour-dispositioned matrons who watched over us like guard hounds.

I neared Plantation House, the magnificent white-columned governor's mansion. The majestic building stood idle and dark, as it had for many years. It was as if it were a glorious crystal chandelier—with all its candles snuffed. I'd always wondered why the East India Company, for which my father was superintendent of public sales, had assigned him to the Briars instead of to the more opulent and unoccupied Plantation House. The thought angered me.

Half a mile to Jamestown, I began to grow weary. I was no longer accustomed to such activity. Running had not been part of the headmistress's prescribed course of study for young ladies!

I regretted that I could not have ridden my horse Belle into Jamestown, but she was suffering from a sore tendon and I did not want to risk laming her. In the future, when she reached maturity, I hoped to run her in the Deadwood Races.

Exhausted, I trudged on.

Jamestowners were ordinarily the last residents of St. Helena to retire each night. The town was a center of unrestrained activity and unchecked impulses. Still, I was surprised at what I heard and saw when I passed the old stone clock tower and arrived in the center of town.

Hundreds of people were dashing to and fro, squealing like greased pigs hunting for cover. I was in danger of being trampled, so I ran into the alleyway next to Porteous' Inn and stood on a fish crate, where I could watch the crowd in relative safety. People were cramming themselves into buildings, struggling to pass six or eight abreast through the narrow doorways. Doors slammed after them, one following another like pistol shots along the long row of brown, wood-frame houses. Heavy padlocks—rarely used on St. Helena—were slapped onto shop entrances by nervous proprietors. Frantic women closed and locked shutters on upstairs windows, pulled down parchment shades, and extinguished their oil lamps. The lights of Jamestown were going out like dying fireflies.

Of those people who remained in the street, most were men; they were shouting and had gathered in a large group. A few held muskets.

I didn't know what to make of all the commotion. No one seemed to be in any condition to be asked what the trouble was. If St. Helena was being attacked, then surely the soldiers would have been alerted. But no soldiers were to be seen. Perhaps it was a slave rebellion, similar to the one Toby told me had broken out on Haiti close to twenty-five years ago.

Then, suddenly, I heard the voice of a small boy coming from behind a rum keg discarded outside the inn. He seemed to be talking to a companion.

I crept nearer and peered over the top of the huge barrel. There were two children—a boy of approximately nine years of age and a younger girl who resembled him and was probably his sister. They were too preoccupied to notice me. They were street urchins, crouched low in their patchwork tatters, faces smeared with grime. The boy was gleefully relating a tale to the girl, who was pale with fright.

"And Boney eats three white goats every day . . . ," the boy said, "and little children. . . ." Trembling, the girl tried to edge away from him, but he caught her by her dirty hair and held her fast. His face took on an even more sinister aspect. "Only English ones," he whispered loudly into her ear. She whimpered. "Only girls!"

The girl screamed, jumped up, and ran down the alley, her brother close at her heels. I laughed, thinking of how many times I had terrified my own younger siblings, Willie and Alexander, with fairy stories. But who was "Boney"? I didn't recall having heard that tale before.

I turned around in time to see one of the Jamestown men passing oil-soaked rags wound on top of sticks to his comrades. Then he touched a burning acacia branch to his stick until the top exploded in orange flame. Though I was standing more than five yards away, I could feel the heat of that torch as it sent thick, black smoke and fumes of burning whale oil into the air. The torch was used to light another—this, another—and on and on through the crowd of men the flame was passed rapidly from torch to torch until all were lit. Then the men marched together in the general direction of the sea. With all the chaos, I'd almost forgotten about the ship's arrival! I wondered whether the men, too, were headed toward her. I followed them.

I gathered my bed jacket closer around me to ward off the cool, coastal breeze. A sizable crowd had gathered on the rocky beach—not just the Jamestowners, but rough-looking types from other parts of the island as well. There were armed soldiers, too: on the beach, up in the hills—I'd never seen so many. They must have been called from their posts all over St. Helena. But why? Were they expecting trouble?

The great ship strained at her anchor in rough seas, three hundred yards offshore. I tried to make out the sea-worn letters on her hull: *N-O-R-T . . . Northumberland!* She was British, to be sure—a tattered Union Jack fluttered from a jackstaff on her bowsprit—and a battleship, at that. At least a dozen guns sprouted from her barnacled sides. *Well,* I reasoned, *at least we aren't being attacked by foreigners.* But what if pirates had taken over the ship?

A large landing boat packed with men and horses

was already on its way from the *Northumberland*. It was still too far away to see any details. The crowd surged toward the water, and the British soldiers, bayonets fixed to their muskets, urged them back.

A leathery old man wearing a buckskin smithy's apron stood next to me, peering out to sea through a spyglass. His face was as red as pomegranate seeds, with deep brown creases around his mouth and neck. He was a Yamstock—a native St. Helenian. They all had that wind-battered look to them. He aimed his glass at the approaching landing boat.

"Who are they?" I asked the Yamstock.

He put his spyglass under his arm and turned to look at me. The man had only one eye! The right socket was empty, and the lid appeared to have been sewn shut.

He cocked his head at a peculiar angle and stared at me a long time, in a way that made me sorry I hadn't thought to change into something more substantial than my nightgown before leaving the Briars.

"Who wants t'know?" he said in a voice halfway between a gargle and a growl.

"Betsy. Betsy Balcombe."

He stared at me again and made a strange

clucking noise with his tongue. "See fer yerself," he said, handing me the spyglass.

I put the cold brass to my eye. The boat and its passengers looked terribly small. I couldn't see any details.

Then, without warning, the Yamstock rudely yanked the glass from my hands. I was stunned and disappointed. Crazy old man!

"Yer got the thing turned wrong way round!" he growled, handing it back to me, this time with the eyepiece facing the proper direction.

"Hmmm . . . ," I said, aiming it at the boat again. I could see the men in the boat very clearly now.

"What d'yer see with those pretty young eyes o'yers?" the Yamstock asked, a bit contemptuously.

"Horses, sailors . . . and oarsmen."

"Aye! Go on."

The moonlight seemed to be fading. I strained to see.

"And . . . officers. One of them's tall . . . gray-haired. With fancy whiskers and uniform."

"Aye. That'd be the adm'ral," the Yamstock said.

"Admiral? Which one?"

"Go on, I say! What else?"

I took the spyglass away from my eye. The Yamstock's bullying was beginning to annoy me.

"Go on!" he snapped.

I scowled at him for his rudeness. Still, I was anxious to learn who was on the boat. So I placed the glass against my eye. I looked through it a long time in silence. A cloud had drifted in front of the moon, and I could no longer see anything worth mentioning. The Yamstock grew impatient with me.

"Well? Well? D'yer see some men what don't look like limeys?"

The clouds shifted again, and the moon shone brightly over the ocean.

This time when I looked at the boat, I noticed a group of men—officers it seemed—I hadn't seen before. They wore strange uniforms. And what was this? There were a few ladies on board too! They wore fancy long dresses of a style unfamiliar to me, and they had silk shawls wrapped around their shoulders. The men and women seemed to be engaged in serious discussion.

"Yes," I said to the Yamstock. "Foreigners. Some ladies, too."

He laughed—an unpleasant, raspy sound.

"Aye!" he said.

I studied the group of foreigners. One man puzzled me. He was small and stood as straight as a measuring stick, but apart from the others, and spoke to no one. No one tried to speak to him. He was the only man on board who was still facing away from the shore. Instead, motionless, hands clasped tightly behind his back, he stared out across the sea. "One of the men—I can't see his face," I said. "He's wearing a big bicorne hat. And he's shorter than the others." "Ahhh!" the Yamstock exulted. "That'd be Boney!" He snatched the spyglass from me and looked through it. Boney. That name again! So he wasn't just a character in a children's fairy tale! He was real. But who was he?

"Is he a pirate?" I asked the Yamstock.

"A pirate?" he said with a snarl, never taking his eye from the glass. "Aye! And a murderer. Ravisher of women, too!"

"Why are they bringing him here?"

The Yamstock turned toward me and glowered with his one eye. "Aye, they should o' hung that little French disease from London Tower and let the rats make short work o' what was left!"

The Yamstock jammed the spyglass into his apron pocket and stomped away, without a word of farewell.

I was tired and eager to return to the Briars. But

having come this far, I was anxious to get a better look at the little Frenchman. I'd never seen a real pirate before!

The clock in Jamestown's stone tower struck the hour. By the first stroke, the landing boat from the *Northumberland* had moored. By the fifth and last stroke, the passengers began to disembark. The order of their exit seemed to have been well planned. First, armed British sailors, sea legs wobbly from their long voyage, tumbled out onto the beach like crabs. As soon as they were able, they formed two neat columns facing each other. Next came navy officers and their orderlies, who helped the foreign ladies out of the boat. The ladies seemed very relieved to be on dry land.

Then, on horseback, came the silver-haired Admiral in his striking black uniform and gold-fringed epaulets. His chest was littered with war medals. He reminded me of the pictures I'd seen of the great English Admiral Nelson, painted to pay tribute to him after he'd died defeating the French at Trafalgar. Of course, unlike Nelson, this fellow had whiskers—and both of his arms.

Then came the foreign officers and orderlies in stiff blue uniforms with red cuffs and white sashes. They waited patiently in formation by the side of the boat. Staring straight ahead, their faces were expressionless.

The crowd of onlookers, which had up to this point watched the scene unfold in near silence, became restless. They began to murmur and press toward the boat. Once more the soldiers held them at bay. The Jamestown men raised their torches high into the air so they could get a better view of the boat. There was a growing sense of anticipation in the air—excitement of an almost tangible sort. I hadn't felt anything like it since the day I'd stood with a crowd outside the palace in London, hoping for a glimpse of the prince regent.

I began to wonder whether there wasn't some member of the royal family aboard. Surely a pirate wasn't worthy of all this attention—not even if he were Jean Lafitte himself! But it was apparent that only one passenger remained aboard: the little Frenchman. Up close he looked even smaller and less impressive than I'd supposed. I was more than a little disappointed. The man was about to mount his horse—a magnificent black charger, trimmed in red and gold—but hesitated. He slid his small, black-booted heel from the stirrup and turned to face the murmuring crowd. As they saw him, they grew louder—more fearful and hostile. The

Jamestown men pushed past the soldiers, gave out a yell—almost a war cry—and marched down the beach to within a few yards of the boat. There they waited and watched.

The crowd's behavior seemed to have a strange and powerful effect upon the Frenchman. He took a slow, deep breath that seemed to infuse him with electric energy. His gray eyes flashed fire; his jaw set in rigid determination. Life flooded into his face and limbs, adding such strength and presence to his appearance that it hardly seemed he could be the same man he was a moment before. He actually seemed to grow taller before my very eyes!

The Frenchman mounted his charger, and the horse stepped onto shore. A few of the Jamestown men shouted things at him that I couldn't understand. Unbeknownst to the British soldiers, one Jamestowner had raised and aimed his musket at the unarmed Frenchman. I tried to yell, but no sound came out. The Frenchman caught sight of the Jamestowner and stared at him with steely intensity. Incredibly, the man lowered his musket as if compelled to do so by an invisible power. Then the Frenchman's gaze swept slowly over the crowd like the beam from a lighthouse. A hush fell upon the crowd. To a man, they fell back, clearing a wide path for the Frenchman. And suddenly, I understood who this man, capable of inspiring such terror, must be.

Bonaparte! Was there any man more feared and hated in all of Europe—in all of history? General Bonaparte. Emperor Bonaparte. What on earth was he doing on St. Helena? Small wonder Jamestown was in such an uproar!

The countries of Europe had been at war with one another for as far back into my childhood as I could remember. I had never known exactly what all the fighting was about. Perhaps, as in most wars, no one really did. But there was one name that was always mentioned in connection with it; one man mocked and condemned again and again in the British gazettes; one name that was never merely spoken, but spat—especially by the London matrons who had lost sons in the war. One man blamed for everything from British debt to British dysentery: Napoleon Bonaparte, emperor of France.

He was rumored to have massacred prisoners of war and even the weak and wounded among his own troops. He was said to have kept a harem in Egypt and a dozen mistresses in every country he conquered. And more than once I'd heard that he'd stolen and sold his wife's jewels to finance his military campaigns. What was fact and what was fiction? I did not know. I'd never paid much attention during Miss Bosworth's history lessons at school. What did I care what happened last week, much less a year or twenty ago? As for the newspapers, only the results of the horse races interested me. I supposed I knew as much of Bonaparte as I cared to—as much as most Englishmen did. And like most my age, I could think back to my childhood and remember the little ditty my mother whispered in my ear as she tucked me in at night:

> *Good night, small one—*
> *Be good and pray*
> *with all your precious heart,*
> *That day will dawn*
> *without a trace*
> *of vicious Boney-parte!*

Ah! So that's where the name "Boney" came from!

It had been only several months since word had come to us in London of Bonaparte's defeat at the Battle of Waterloo; I was sure I'd heard the last of him. I recall at the time some of the girls at Hawthorne were discussing possible methods of disposing of him. One of them actually proposed baking him into a tureen of French liver pâté and serving him to King George! And now, these several months later, it occurred to me that perhaps St. Helena was, in a sense, serving as that tureen. Perhaps this was the King's chosen method of disposing of the vanquished Emperor Napoleon. Not a bad choice, at that. If I had an enemy I wished to see rot, I'd ship him posthaste to St. Helena!

The long procession from the *Northumberland* wended its way up the beach. Bonaparte on his charger passed by close enough for me to smell the horse sweat. His face and body were brilliantly illuminated by the torches of the Jamestowners who lined his path. He looked not unlike the portraits I'd seen of him in London. Oh, he was a bit fatter, and I was surprised to see how yellowish and waxy the skin on his plump, round face appeared. But then, most portraits tend to flatter their subject. The short, green military jacket with red collar and piping, the fine white linen vest and breeches, the cumbersome black hat that seemed a bit too large for his small features, even the silver Star of Honor pinned to his breast—all were precisely as depicted in the gallery portraits and newspaper engravings. Bonaparte's eagle eyes stared straight ahead seeming to see everyone— and yet no one—as he advanced through the silent crowd. For their part, their attention was fixed solely on the emperor. No one took any notice of the British admiral nor of any of the others. Where, I wondered, was the admiral taking him? By the look of things, it was difficult to determine just who was leading whom!

Not long before the sun began to peek over the mountains on St. Helena, the procession passed from my view. I was suddenly too weary to follow.

It was so far to the Briars that I decided to sleep out a few hours and return home as soon as I awoke. I was accustomed to doing this and to slipping back into the Briars unnoticed. Mercifully, my family were late risers. As long as I returned before ten o'clock, they'd be none the wiser.

I had little trouble finding a proper bed. Next to a barn, not far from the beach, stood a rusty wheelbarrow—just my size! And now, for a mattress: I loaded the barrow with hay, which I'd pulled from the bales stacked nearby. Then I climbed aboard. I daresay it made a finer resting place than that "bed of nails" they gave me at Hawthorne!

I watched the last star of night fade into the sunrise. Then I shut my eyes and thought about my encounter with Emperor Napoleon. *Too bad,* I mused, *I can't tell Jane about it.* I couldn't trust her to keep mum. And besides, I could imagine just how she'd react. I'd tell her the whole incredible story of my adventure, including the fact that I'd stood near enough to the most feared man on earth to have reached out and touched him. And what would Jane say? *Good heavens, Betsy! You slept in a wheelbarrow?*

I laughed myself to sleep.

Chapter 3

I'm certain I would have slept half the day away if a game hen hadn't seen fit to use my belly as her roost. She pounced on me, and I was jarred from a deep sleep—not a pleasant experience, to be sure. Despite a few aches and pains in my wheelbarrow-cramped limbs, I chased her all the way to the ocean, knowing the next wave would drench her from beak to bottom. A moment later the origin of the saying "mad as a wet hen" was no longer a mystery to me. Ah, sweet revenge!

Self-satisfaction melted away quickly as I noted the position of the sun in the sky. My worst fears were confirmed when I heard the toll of the Jamestown clock: seven . . . eight . . . nine bells. Nine o'clock already!

I fell down twice, scratched my cheek on a nettle, and tore the hem of my nightgown in the mad dash to reach home before my parents awoke. Still, I got there more quickly than ever before.

All was quiet outside the Briars. I was in luck. Normally, my father would have been in the fields by this time, giving the day's instructions to the slave overseer. If my father found out I'd been out all night, he might have sent me back to Hawthorne for another year!

I ran around to the back of the house and climbed up the vine to my bedroom. *Blast!* The window was stuck. No, not stuck. Locked! Damn that miserable creature, she'd locked me out. I would have cursed Jane through the glass, but she wasn't even in our room. I had no choice but to climb back down and go around to the front entrance.

I said a quick prayer on the threshold: "Please, please let them be asleep!" Then, quietly, hardly daring to breathe, I opened the heavy oak door a crack and peered inside.

I couldn't see anyone, but I heard voices coming from another part of the house. With any luck, I could slip upstairs unnoticed. I galloped across the bright Persian rug in the parlor—and came within inches of colliding with a man who roared *"Zut alors!"*

as I whizzed past. I stopped dead in my tracks and turned around to find myself face-to-face with Napoleon Bonaparte.

Somehow, I had the presence of mind to behave as if there were nothing the slightest bit out of the ordinary in finding him here. I spoke to him in French, the only subject I'd excelled in at school.

"*Pardonnez-moi,* monsieur," I said.

He looked me over from head to toe as if I were a heifer he was thinking of purchasing at market. He seemed to take particular note of my bare feet and ragged nightgown.

"Hmmfftt!" he said—that was all. Then he waved the back of his small, white, plump hand at me, as if he were shooing flies.

Apparently, I was being dismissed from his presence. More than happy to oblige him, I ran up the stairs three at a time and then into my bedroom. I shut the door behind me. Finally!—a chance to think. I paced up and down the creaky wooden floorboards.

The first thing to do, I reasoned, was to change into my day clothes. After all, assuming Bonaparte hadn't done away with my parents, I was still in danger of their punishing me should they discover I'd been out all night. Forgoing the scratchy petticoats my mother always pleaded with me to wear, I slipped directly into my only clean frock: a frilly pink cotton nonsense that Jane had outgrown and handed down to me. How I hated it!

One glance in the looking glass told me that I ought to try to make some sense of my hair. My pale golden curls stood out at odd angles like celery roots. Unfortunately, I didn't have the faintest idea what to do about it. Jane or one of the older girls at Hawthorne had always arranged my hair for me. "You're so helpless, Betsy!"—or was it "hopeless"?—Jane often said to me. But I could find better things to do with my time than fussing with curling irons.

I shook my head like a wet spaniel until a few pieces of hay fluttered to the floor. Then I pinned all my hair in a pile on top of my head. *Good enough,* I thought, and headed for the door. I was about to go downstairs but thought better of it. I realized it would be best if I learned more of what was going on at the Briars before I made my presence known. Taking care not to get soot on my frock, I removed the screen from the fireplace and climbed inside. By the time I was four years old, I'd made the happy discovery that the chimney led directly from the library to my bedroom and that conversations in one room could be heard distinctly in the other. I listened.

The first thing I heard was a sound as familiar to me as the plaintive wail of St. Helena's seagulls. My mother was weeping. This in itself was not cause for alarm—she cried over everything and nothing. But it spurred my curiosity. There was also an undercurrent of rapping noises, occurring in short bursts at frequent intervals, like percussive accompaniment to the melodic theme of tears. This I recognized as my father nervously rapping his pipe against the fireplace to empty it of old tobacco. He always did this when my mother wept, probably because he felt bewildered by it and inadequate to the task of comforting her.

"Hear him out, my dear. Hear him out," I heard my father say, clearly discomfited.

Then a man—of fine old British stock, I judged by his manner of speech—joined the conversation. He cleared his throat, as if rather more out of uneasiness than any trace of influenza.

"May I offer you my sincere apologies, Mrs. Balcombe, for—for causing you such discomfort. I'm sure I handled the situation rather badly."

"Not at all, Admiral," I heard my father say. "Not at all."

So, the man was an admiral. The one from the *Northumberland*, no doubt.

At this point my mother said something, but as she still had tears in her voice, I could not make it out. In any case, the admiral replied, "It would only be for a few months. Until we can find a proper place for him elsewhere on St. Helena."

At this, I began to suspect the nature of the proposal the admiral must have made to my parents.

"Bonaparte has been known to vanquish entire nations in less time, Admiral," my father said sternly.

"I assure you, Balcombe, I have just spent seventy days at sea with the man. Without his army, he is not a dangerous fellow."

My father replied with a skeptical "Harumph."

"We have children, Admiral Cockburn," my mother said calmly. "Two of them are young ladies," she said meaningfully. I could picture her now, dry-eyed and alert, regally maternal, sitting up as straight as a washboard in her chair.

"Madam, I understand your concern. He will be watched day and night—his every move. Over two thousand British soldiers are charged with supervising his captivity. Five hundred guns stand aready. I give you my word that—"

"And you say this is not a dangerous man!" my mother interrupted.

"To France, perhaps. To England, certainly. But to you?" The admiral probably shrugged, allowing his question to hang in the air like chimney dust. There was a silence. Then he tried a new tack. "Balcombe, you and I served together at sea," he said earnestly. "Men who have shared berth and battle don't steer each other wrong on dry land."

Another silence followed, this one longer than the last.

My father sighed, just the way he does when I wheedle him for pin money and he's ready for surrender. "He's right, my dear," my father said wearily. "The admiral would not allow us to place ourselves in any danger. We must do as he asks."

"Whatever you think best," my mother said, her voice heavy with resignation. It was like her to give in without a fight. From whom did I inherit my pluck?

Just then I heard the approach of smooth and graceful footsteps—as those of a lady. Someone had joined the group in the library.

"I see I am no longer in any danger of being washed away by madame's tears," Bonaparte said. "Your aides saw to it that my sortie was as brief as it was well supervised."

Hmmm, I thought. *There must be some officers about, whom I missed seeing on my way into the house.*

"But they were pleasant company, I trust?" the admiral said, a bit of mischief in his tone.

"Oh, quite pleasant, Admiral," he replied. "If a bit too familiar."

The man's English was abominable. I untangle it here with difficulty.

My legs were growing weary of holding the same uncomfortable position for so long. I shifted my weight from one foot to the other, which stirred up some soot. Try as I might—and, oh, how I did try!—I couldn't contain a sneeze.

"God bless you, my dear," I heard my father say.

"I didn't sneeze," my mother replied puzzledly.

I stifled a giggle in my fist lest they hear that as well.

There was some awkward small talk for a moment or two. It was clear just how ill at ease my parents felt with Bonaparte in the room. Then my father said solemnly: "I think it's time we call the children."

"Jane is out with the boys," my mother said. "They should return shortly. Have you seen Betsy this morning?"

"No," my father replied, uneasiness creeping into his forthright manner. I knew he was wondering whether I'd gotten myself into some sort of mischief.

"I'll call upstairs for her. You'll excuse me, gentlemen?"

My mother's rapid exit alerted me to move quickly if I hoped to avoid being caught eavesdropping.

"Betsy!" she called from the parlor.

I leaped out of the fireplace, bumping my head in the process. "Ow! . . . er . . . yes, Mother?" I called back.

"Betsy, are you quite all right?"

"Yes, Mother." I brushed the soot from my dress.

"Then come downstairs, please. We have guests in the library."

I could tell she was going to great lengths to conceal the quaver in her voice.

As I entered the library, I was surprised to see that Jane and my brothers were present, having just returned from their outing. Willie and little Alexander were too young to recognize Bonaparte on sight, and Jane too ignorant. I smiled inwardly, anticipating the unpleasant surprise in store for her.

My mother was serving tea and cakes. Her hands shook so much, the fine china cups rattled like bones on the tray. Bonaparte stood by himself, absorbed in removing some of my father's books from the shelves and examining them. My father and the admiral chatted amiably, reminiscing about their days at sea.

I was about to make myself comfortable on the settee, but my mother caught my eye and shook her head vigorously at me. Reluctantly, I continued to stand.

"Won't you sit down, monsieur?" my mother said nervously, offering Bonaparte my place on the sofa.

He either did not hear or chose to ignore her. In any case, he made no reply.

"Monsieur?" my mother ventured timidly.

Slowly, he turned around. Bonaparte first looked puzzled, then extremely annoyed. The transformation was sudden and complete. "You are addressing me, madame?" he snapped.

My mother was taken aback. Jane looked stricken. My father and the admiral ceased their conversation.

My mother plucked up her courage and nodded at Bonaparte.

"Madame, if we are to live under the same roof, then I suggest you learn to address me in a more appropriate manner." He did not elaborate. My mother nodded like a small child who'd received a scolding from her teacher. So, just as

I'd thought: He was moving in with us!

An uncomfortable silence ensued. Then the admiral attempted to lighten the atmosphere. He held up a tea cake, cleared his throat, and said: "Mrs. Balcombe, these are marvelous. If you can make hardtack and boiled sow as well as you can tea cakes, there's a place for you on my ship!"

She smiled wanly in appreciation. My father chuckled.

"Sorry, Admiral," my father said. "My wife has her own crew to cook for."

"Understood, Captain Balcombe," the admiral replied, smiling.

"William?" my mother said, as a reminder to my father that there was business at hand. He caught her meaning.

"Children," he said, "gather round. Gather round." He pointed to an area on the rug.

Jane, Willie, and Alexander lined up in front of the stern-faced Bonaparte, who stood at attention, hands folded behind his back. My brothers and sister seemed unsure of whether to expect an inspection or a firing squad.

"You too, Betsy," my father added when he saw I was laggard. I took my place in line.

"Children, this gentleman will be our guest for

a while. General Bonaparte, these are our children. Jane . . ."

Gleefully, I noted that Jane was turning as pale as pastry flour. Bonaparte nodded at her to acknowledge the introduction. She staggered a bit, then took a step backward in an attempt to conceal this. She curtsied and managed to croak out: "*Bon— Bonjour*, monsieur."

Next, my father turned his attention to the boys. "William Junior," he said. "And Alexander."

"It's vicious Boney-parte!" the terrified Alexander whispered into his older brother's ear— loud enough, unfortunately, for everyone to hear. My father turned purple with embarrassment. Little Alexander clung to Willie, gripping his waist so tightly from behind that poor Willie swayed back and forth like a dinghy. Alexander peeked out from behind his brother.

I studied Bonaparte's face, and I could swear that I saw the trace of an amused smile appear on his lips as he watched the trembling boys. He took one step toward them, and they cowered all the more. Then, quickly, Bonaparte mussed up his hair with the tips of his fingers and bugged out his eyes like an ogre. He bent down low and leaned close to them. "Argghh!" he growled.

The boys screamed and jumped back in terror. This frightened Jane, who fell backward right into a pile of ashes in the fireplace! She wasn't hurt—only her pride, I suppose. My father helped her up.

Bonaparte laughed wickedly. I laughed too, I confess. Bonaparte noticed my reaction and seemed intrigued by it. My mother glowered at me in disapproval.

"Now, was that really necessary, sir?" said the admiral to Bonaparte, attempting to be stern. But, really, it was obvious the admiral was as amused as I.

My father did his best to overlook the incident, but I noticed that he did not look at Bonaparte when, a moment later, he presented me to him.

"This is our daughter Elizabeth," he said. "We call her Betsy."

"*Je suis très heureuse de faire vôtre connaissance,* Your Majesty," I said, bowing my head slightly since curtsying did not suit me.

Bonaparte raised an eyebrow and looked at me with an odd combination of agreeable surprise and suspicion. I suppose he wasn't certain whether I was being respectful or subtly mocking him. I watched as his small gray eyes narrowed into lizardly slits of concentration. Then he scrutinized my face feature by feature, like a gypsy fortune-teller reading tea leaves. I realized that he was wondering why I looked so familiar to him.

"We have met before, you and I . . . ," he mused.

"No, sir. That is, I don't see how that would be possible, sir," I lied, hoping against hope that he wouldn't recognize me as the girl who'd nearly run him over in the parlor.

"I'm sure mademoiselle must be correct," he said with formality.

I would have felt relieved at hearing this, but his manner was disturbingly ambiguous. It was impossible for me to judge his sincerity by his expression.

Then, quite unexpectedly, he demanded to be left alone with me. Naturally, my mother was mortified. She rose instantly from her chair to protest. But, somehow, my father managed to stop her before she voiced her objection, in that mysterious way married people have of communicating their desires without saying a single word.

My family and the admiral filed quickly out of the room without ceremony, like good soldiers given the order to break ranks. Frankly, I resented their unquestioning obedience to Bonaparte's wishes.

Was I worth so little to my parents that they would hand me over to anyone, however disreputable, who took the trouble to ask? It would serve them right if Bonaparte took this opportunity to bludgeon me with the coatrack or the andirons!

For the moment, however, the man seemed to have entirely forgotten that I was in the room with him. He walked briskly about the library, freely picking up and examining all of dozens of objects that took his fancy. His curiosity bordered on gluttony. It was immediately apparent to me that his mind functioned at an almost unimaginable pace, swallowing information as voraciously as a shark devours its prey. Though the room was crammed to overflowing with books, objets d'art, and my father's nautical memorabilia, Bonaparte managed to navigate through the sea of articles with startling speed and efficiency. He did not damage or misplace anything. I noted that he was able to collect half a dozen or more items at once from different locations in the room, study them, then return each to its proper place, seemingly without a moment's thought or hesitation.

He seemed particularly fascinated by my father's old navy sword, which hung from worn leather thongs over the fireplace, and two ship models: of Admiral Nelson's frigate, the *Victory*, and Admiral Collingwood's *Royal Sovereign*.

Once he'd satisfied his curiosity about the contents of the room, he moved toward the south window overlooking Toby's rose garden. The morning sunlight streamed through the glass, making rainbows in the bell jars that covered my father's ship models. Bonaparte placed himself directly in the path of the sunlight. He took off his big bicorne hat—he'd been rude enough to have worn it inside the house—placed it under his arm, and stared out the window. In a moment he seemed to have entered a trance.

By this time I had grown very impatient with the man and was anxious to leave. He was so eerily absorbed in his daydreaming that I was certain he would not notice my exit. I headed for the door.

"It is very quiet," he said, startling me. I wasn't sure whether he had directed his remark at me or at himself, but I decided that I ought not leave just yet. I risked a reply.

"We are in the country, sir."

He continued to stare out the window. I was not accustomed to holding a conversation with a man's backbone. I made for the door once more.

"You speak French well," he said crisply. "Better than the others."

This remark drew me back. He was silent for a moment, and I got the impression that he was waiting for me to return the compliment. How ridiculous! *Surely*, I thought, *he must know his English is dreadful.*

"I've only just returned from school," I said diplomatically.

"From school . . . ," he mused. Then, with appalling speed and suddenness, he fired questions at me like a barrage of artillery. I battled to keep apace.

"What is the capital of France?" he ordered.

"Paris."

"Of Italy?"

"Rome."

"Russia?"

"Petersburg now," I said, breathless. "Moscow formerly."

Then, abruptly, he turned to face me. His fists were clenched white, eyes like two long gray pins fixing me where I stood. He was agitated, electrified— almost mad, really. The nervous twitching of his left thigh muscle caught my eye.

"Qui l'a brûlée?" he demanded.

I was stunned by his senseless intensity, struck dumb by it.

"Who burned it?!" he roared, slamming his fist on the desk. The bell jars rattled with the force of the blow.

"I—I don't know, sir," I said.

"Mais oui!" he said with a laugh. "You know very well. I did!"

So. He burned Moscow, just as he'd destroyed so much else with his battles and conquests. What was I to say? *Jolly good show*?

Bonaparte delighted in his own cleverness, chuckling heartily. All signs of anger and agitation instantly vanished from his features. He was merry, lighthearted. He didn't even seem to notice that I was not laughing with him.

How could I have laughed? The change in his behavior was too sudden, too sweeping. I began to wonder about the angry scene I had witnessed only moments before. Was it playacting? Was he merely testing me?

Bonaparte sat down in the chair behind my father's desk. He drummed his fingers nervously on the desktop and looked straight at me. "Why did you try to deceive me?" he said.

"Sir?" I didn't know what he meant.

"We met in the drawing room," he said. "You are not a very good liar."

"I—I try to be, sir."

He laughed. "Never mind. I have had more practice at it than you."

I looked at him, not knowing quite what to say. It didn't matter; by now his attention was occupied elsewhere.

From his position at the desk, he could see out another of the library's windows. This one had a view of dark boulders streaked with brackish water from underground wellsprings like greenish blood. Instead of trees and grasses, there was a barren and colorless expanse; volcanic ash and pumice stretched as far as the eye could see, long since having beaten all life into dreary submission. And instead of gently rolling hills, there was a row of terrible, sharp mountains, jutting like fangs from the jaw of a leviathan.

Bonaparte was transfixed by the melancholy landscape. I supposed that he was thinking about what life would be like for him now—his life as a captive on St. Helena. He muttered something very quietly to himself, as one does in dreaming. I doubted he was aware he'd said anything aloud.

"The Bastille was a kinder prison . . . ," he said.

I stood for a few moments more, waiting for him to dismiss me. He seemed so deep in thought that I didn't dare disturb him.

I let myself out.

Chapter 4

Bonaparte spent the night at Porteous' Inn in Jamestown—a fact that Admiral Cockburn took great pains to conceal from its nervous citizens.

The next morning Bonaparte moved into the Briars. Or, rather, "Bonaparte & Company" did. He was accompanied by a suite of French officers and their wives—aristocrats, mostly—as well as his personal servants, chefs, and valets. They had all sailed with Bonaparte on the *Northumberland* after he was taken prisoner by the English. I'm not sure how my parents felt about putting up so many unexpected guests, and such odd ones at that, but they did their best to conceal any resentment they may have felt.

There wasn't room for the exiles in the main

part of the house, so my father set them up in the Pavilion. The Pavilion was a house detached from the rest of the Briars but only a few steps away. We'd used it to house high-ranking visitors in the past, including Bonaparte's nemesis, the Duke of Wellington, who'd sent him down to defeat at Waterloo.

I watched in amazement as crate after crate of Bonaparte's belongings was carried into the house. There was an endless stream of them. Some of the boxes were so large that they had to be turned on their sides in order to fit through the door. My father had called in some of his field hands to assist, and they worked side by side with Bonaparte's men. No one but the ladies and the emperor himself was exempt from carrying crates. Bonaparte oversaw the whole operation as if he were commanding in battle, dividing up responsibilities, coordinating flanks, and shouting, *"Vite!* Quickly!" to rouse failing spirits. It was a strange sight to see— dignified French officers transporting goods on their backs like pack mules.

Most seemed to take the situation in stride, but a few did not. One man complained constantly and bitterly about everything: his aching feet and back, the arduousness of his task and its inappropriateness to one of his high station. He bemoaned the heat of the day, which seemed to me a particularly ridiculous complaint since he was so obviously overdressed for the weather. A bit of a dandy, I thought. A fop. I took an instant dislike to him.

The man half dropped one of the crates on the Pavilion doorstep with an "ooph!" and a thud. Then he grimaced, gripped his lower back, and limped— rather too theatrically, it seemed to me—toward the emperor.

"Sire," he whined, "I am happy to serve His Majesty in whatever capacity he sees fit. But if I am crippled with the lumbago, I will unfortunately be deprived of the pleasure of serving him in the future!"

"Now, now, Gourgaud," Bonaparte replied, humoring him. "We've been at sea a long time. The exercise will do you good."

"But, Sire—"

"Ah-ah-ah!" Bonaparte said, raising his index finger. "You must set a good example for the others, Gourgaud. They all look up to you, you know."

Gourgaud seemed very pleased by this trans- parent flattery. His chest puffed up with pride until the ruffles on his shirtfront stood out like pheasant's plumage. He rejoined the work detail.

About a quarter of an hour later Bonaparte made an announcement. "Messieurs," he said, "it is time for a rest." He pointed to several of the slaves. "You—you, there!—you, you, and you. You will take a respite. *Dix minutes—c'est tout!* The remainder of you will have your rest once they return."

Gourgaud, who, of course, was not among those selected for the first ten-minute rest period, huffed toward the emperor, his long puffy shirtsleeves flapping in the breeze. He was red in the face, sputtering like a teakettle. "Sire! Sire, forgive me for speaking so boldly, but—but I cannot understand why you have allowed these Negroes to take a respite ahead of me! After all, they are merely slaves. They are used to performing manual labor. Whereas I—"

"Assez!" the emperor snapped. "We are guests here!"

Gourgaud stood quietly.

"You are correct that these men are slaves," the emperor said brittlely. "When we are finished with them here, they must toil again all day in the fields while you retreat to a warm bath and a good meal. All the more reason why they should have a rest before you!"

I was more than a little surprised by Bonaparte's remarks. I would not have expected that he'd have any compassion for his social inferiors, since he'd demonstrated so little for his equals. As for me, I'd never had any stomach for slavery. I'd seen one too many of those execrable floating dungeons we call "slave ships" from Guinea and Angola sail into Jamestown Harbor with their wretched human cargo in chains. It had always troubled me that my family kept slaves. We were no different from other reasonably well-to-do families on St. Helena in that respect, but to me, this did not lessen the offense. On several occasions I'd tried to convince my father to free our slaves, but my efforts were in vain. He'd always tap his pipe nervously in the palm of his hand when I brought up the subject, explaining that while he deplored slavery as much as I, there were no other laborers on the island who had the necessary skills to tend our yam fields and could be hired at reasonable cost and that, in any case, he was sure our slaves were better treated than most paid workers on St. Helena. While this may have been true, I still felt my father's attitude was rather hypocritical. Of course, I did not tell him so.

It was not long after Monsieur Gourgaud grumblingly returned to the work brigade that I heard my mother call me from the house. By tradition, I never answered her before the third "Bet-see!" and this time was no exception.

"Yes?" I called back at last. She poked her head out of a downstairs window.

"Yes, who?" my father said to me as he approached.

He was returning from a hunt carrying his musket, and had the dogs with him. They yapped busily at his heels.

"Yes, who?" he said again.

"Catch anything?" I asked, evading his question. I grinned at him slyly because I knew full well he hadn't bagged so much as a sparrow. My father wasn't much of a shot. He tried to frown, but a bit of a smile showed through. This was a game we often played.

"Never mind that now, Miss Balcombe," he said teasingly. "Your mother is calling you. Yes, who?" I stifled a groan.

"Yes, Mother," I said, giving in. We'd been through this procedure umpteen times; I felt I was really getting a bit old for it.

"Much better, young woman," he said. He bent down and patted our dog Tom Pipes on the muzzle. "And to you, sir," he said to the dog, "better luck

49

next time. Where's that grouse you promised me? A gentleman always keeps his promises, sir."

I laughed. My father was in a surprisingly good mood, considering he'd just returned from hunting. He looked at me. "Go and see what your mother needs," he said.

When I returned outside shortly thereafter, to relay the message my mother had asked me to convey to the emperor, Bonaparte was nowhere to be seen. In fact, the area in front of the Pavilion was deserted. Bonaparte and his suite were probably inside. I wondered what I should do.

I stood for a few moments on the doorstep of the Pavilion, listening to the call of the mynah birds in the distance. *Would it be all right if I knocked on the door?* I wondered. I stood there dumbly, hesitant, as the birds mocked me. *How absurd,* I thought. *Here I am on the doorstep of my own home, and I'm behaving as if I were a wandering beggar!* I knocked loudly, then reached for the doorknob. My hand snatched only the air; someone had opened the door.

"*Oui?*" Gourgaud inquired superciliously. He looked me over, making no effort to conceal his contempt. I stood up as tall as I could.

"I have a message for the emperor," I said.

"Who are you?"

"Betsy Balcombe."

Gourgaud frowned and tugged at his lacy cuffs. "His Majesty does not wish to be disturbed."

He seemed about to shut the door in my face, so I spoke quickly. "The message is from my mother, who has been kind enough to provide the emperor with a place to stay."

Gourgaud sighed loudly and crossed his arms impatiently. "You may give your message to me," he said.

"My mother has asked me to give the message to the emperor."

Gourgaud stared at me for a moment, surprised, I suppose, by my persistence. "His Majesty does not wish to be disturbed," he said with finality, pushing the door toward the jamb. I had to jump backward in order to avoid getting my nose smashed by it. *Blast the blackguard!*

"Gourgaud, *qui est là?*" a voice called from inside the Pavilion.

Gourgaud froze; the half-shut door stayed where it was. "*Personne*, Sire!" he called back.

Nobody? The arrogance of the man!

I couldn't quite make out his French, but Bonaparte then said something to the effect of:

"Nonsense, Gourgaud! Nobodies don't knock on doors. Find out who it is."

Gourgaud's shoulders sank.

"*Est-ce qu'un homme ou une femme?*" the emperor called.

Gourgaud, flustered, made no reply.

"Gourgaud! *Parlez!*"

"*C'est . . . c'est une femme*, Sire. A young lady," he called. Then, after looking at me disdainfully: "*Je suppose . . .*"

"Ahhh!" the emperor exulted, as if anticipating a "conquest." "*En ce cas . . . entrez*, madame!"

I smirked triumphantly at Gourgaud. With great reluctance, he opened the door and led me up to the emperor's chambers.

The emperor was holding court from his bath. He sat in a great iron tub—the length of two men—which rested on four gargoyle feet in the center of the room he'd chosen as his bedchamber. The tub was filled with hot water, steam rising from it like rings of pipe smoke. But instead of tobacco, the scent of sandalwood soap filled my nostrils. Presumably, the emperor was quite naked; but from where I stood, I could see only those parts of him that were above the waterline.

The hair on the emperor's head and chest was

chestnut-colored, pressed close and flat against his plump body by steam and sweat. His skin was startlingly white and looked as soft as a lady's. Overall, he resembled nothing so much as my mother's steamed potato dumplings. Still, his nose was straight and regal, the small nostrils curling delicately like two apostrophes. And his dimpled hands, which rested on the sides of the iron tub, were small and elegant like those of a master violincellist. Even seated, the emperor's back remained straight as a ramrod. So, despite his plumpness, his appearance could not have been called unkingly.

Gourgaud and I had entered the room cautiously; the emperor had not yet noticed us. He was busily giving orders to a young valet who, using buckets of hot and cold water, was doing his best to maintain the bath at a temperature to His Majesty's liking. But there seemed no pleasing him. At the emperor's request the valet added more cold water to the bath.

"Brrrr! *Trop froid!*" Bonaparte complained.

The valet promptly picked up another of the buckets and poured hot water into the tub.

"*Arrêtez*, Marchand!" the emperor roared, stopping him. "*Trop chaud!*" The gentle Marchand, a handsome fellow with curly blond hair and smiling azure eyes, seemed to have infinite patience with his emperor's fickle demands.

In addition to Marchand, two other attendants were present: a stooped, bespectacled old man who sat, quill in hand, at a writing desk; and a gaunt, unattractive boy who was perhaps a year younger than I and bore an unfortunate family resemblance to the old scribe. The boy was perched on a high stool, his long bony legs dangling like he was a heron caught in a tree; he stole moonstruck glances my way that irked me.

Gourgaud cleared his throat and stood at attention. "Sire," Gourgaud announced, "Mademoiselle . . . er . . ."

"Betsy," I supplied, annoyed.

"Mademoiselle Betsy," Gourgaud proclaimed. He spun on his heel and marched from the room.

Bonaparte turned to look at me. His anticipatory smile promptly fell from his face, and his eyes widened in astonishment. I was clearly not the sort of visitor he'd hoped for.

"Who gave you permission to enter?" the emperor demanded.

"You did, sir," I said.

His cheek muscles twitched, but he said nothing. Without a moment's pause, he turned toward the old man and said, "Where were we, Las Cases? Read it back to me."

Las Cases adjusted the spectacles on his nose, picked up a document from the desk, and read aloud: "'A letter to His Majesty, King George III of England. No—better make that to the prince regent. They tell me the old scoundrel's so addled, he doesn't know his crown from his—'"

"Diable!" Bonaparte swore, splashing about angrily in his tub. "You fool!"

"What's wrong, Your Majesty?" Las Cases asked.

"Oh . . . never mind!" Bonaparte sighed, trying to regain his composure. "We begin again," he said. "To His Majesty, the Prince Regent of England." The emperor dictated rapidly. Poor Las Cases scribbled in a race to keep up with him, his pen scratching on the paper like chickens hunting for grubs in the barnyard. "Your Royal Highness: Some months ago, I came to England to throw myself upon the hospitality of the British people and place myself under the protection of their laws. I anticipated a fate just and reasonable, befitting my exalted position. I expected no less from Your Majesty as the most powerful, the most constant, and the most generous of my enemies.

"Instead, I was condemned to ignominy on this island, a miserable wart on the face of the deep.

"The monarchs of Europe, whether friends or foes, are brothers by virtue of their common bonds of sacrosanct authority. It is not possible to debase one imperial brother without similarly diminishing all the others. The peoples under their dominion, if taught to disrespect one sovereign, will learn to disregard them all.

"Your Majesty, I hold that my defeat is your defeat. My humiliation is your humiliation. And, in the end, if I am not recalled from this foul prison, my fate also will be yours."

The emperor fell silent. After a moment he said, "The usual closing, Las Cases."

Las Cases scribbled a few more lines and sprinkled blotting sand on the paper. He placed the letter, a silver ink bottle, and a quill on a silver tray, which was carried to the emperor by the boy. Ceremoniously, the boy dipped the quill into the ink, then handed it to the emperor to sign the document. Apparently, the boy was kept on solely to perform that one, trifling task. I thought it a ridiculous extravagance.

After he'd signed the letter, Bonaparte looked around, and his eyes fell upon me. He frowned.

"Well?" he demanded impatiently, as if I'd been keeping him waiting.

"I have a message from my mother for you, sir."

"Well?"

"She wishes to know if you would join us for supper today."

He burst out laughing. Rather rude of him, I thought, but I ignored it.

"Shall we expect you, then?"

Bonaparte laughed even louder. Confused, I looked questioningly at Marchand.

"The emperor does not dine with others, mademoiselle," Marchand kindly explained. "They dine with *him*. And then, only at His Majesty's invitation."

Marchand looked at the emperor expectantly. He seemed to be hoping that his master would invite my mother to supper.

"My robe, Marchand," was all the emperor said. I can't say I was surprised that no invitation was forthcoming.

Bonaparte began to stand up in his bath, heedless of the fact that a female was present. Marchand rushed forward with an Oriental bamboo screen to conceal him as he stepped from the tub.

The afternoon sunlight flooded through a tall window behind the emperor. I could see his dark, rotund outline through the screen as Marchand helped him on with his robe. The effect reminded me of those black paper silhouettes cut by the sidewalk artists of London.

The emperor's silhouette shuddered. "Shut that window, Marchand! There's a draft."

Marchand obliged him.

Resplendent in his crimson velvet robe, the emperor stepped out from behind the screen. He shivered. "This drafty tomb will make me nostalgic for the Russian winter," he said acidly, directing his remarks at me.

"I hope you will be comfortable, sir." I said. "Most visitors like the Pavilion. Of course, they are usually soldiers and sailors."

"And what am I, pray?"

"An emperor," I said. I did not intend to pay him any compliment by this, I was merely stating a fact. But he nonetheless seemed pleased by my remark.

"In the past," I added, "our visitors have been on active service."

His smile instantly evaporated. "I, too, have been on active service," he said.

There was a knock on the front door, and a moment later Gourgaud entered the room.

"What is it, Gourgaud?" the emperor said.

"Forgive the interruption, Sire. Admiral Cockburn is here. He says he wishes to see General Bonaparte about a matter of some importance."

The emperor scowled and turned toward the wall. "Tell the admiral that as far as I know, 'General' Bonaparte was last seen fighting the Mamelukes in Egypt! If he wishes to see the emperor, that is another matter entirely."

Gourgaud smirked approvingly at the emperor's insistence upon protocol. He bowed and exited, returning a few moments later looking a bit dejected. "He says it is important, Sire."

We all waited to see what the emperor would do next.

"Very well, Gourgaud," he said at last. "Show him in."

Admiral Cockburn entered with the brisk military gait I'd seen so often among my father's naval friends. My father no longer walked that way since he'd developed the gout.

Cockburn stood in front of the emperor, who was now sitting in a chair at the end of the room. By his lofty manner, Bonaparte managed to turn that chair into a throne, and the admiral had to muster all his dignity so as not to seem like a peon.

Cockburn took off his hat and nodded respectfully at Bonaparte.

"General," Cockburn acknowledged.

"Good afternoon, Lieutenant," replied Bonaparte.

The admiral looked puzzled. He stroked his silver whiskers. "You mistake my rank, sir," he said.

"And you, mine," the emperor said brusquely.

The admiral smiled slightly and said nothing. I guessed that this wasn't the first time they'd locked horns over the admiral's refusal to call him "Your Majesty." This round appeared to be a victory for the emperor.

After a moment Bonaparte nodded at Marchand, who offered the admiral a chair. Cockburn sat down.

"You will be subject to certain rules and regulations while you are under my supervision," the admiral began. "I see no reason to delay in informing you of them." Cockburn then glanced at me uncomfortably. "Miss Balcombe, I believe your father said he was looking for you."

"I just spoke to him, sir," I said, refusing to take the hint.

One thing I could count on: Whenever adults tried to evict me from a room, the conversation was about to become interesting. I stood there with the innocent look on my face I'd perfected during my years as a desperado at Hawthorne.

"Miss Balcombe . . . ," the admiral admonished. Reluctantly, I turned to go.

"Mademoiselle may stay," the emperor intervened, much to my surprise. "I may need a witness, one day."

"A witness?" Cockburn asked. "To what?"

"My imprisonment is a crime," he replied. "One is always better off having witnesses when a crime is committed. *N'est-ce pas?*"

The admiral did not respond, but he accepted my presence without further dispute. No one invited me to sit down, so I leaned against the fireplace and prepared to listen.

"You and your suite will stay at the Pavilion until construction is completed at Longwood," the admiral said to Bonaparte. I knew Longwood House. It was a dilapidated structure a few miles from the Briars. It had once been owned by the East India Company, but no one had lived in it for years.

"Longwood should be ready for you sometime after the arrival of the new governor," the admiral continued. "He will take over my responsibilities of overseeing your captivity."

Bonaparte listened without comment.

I wished I could have asked the admiral about the new governor. I wanted to know whether he had any daughters my age. It would be nice to have someone to talk to besides Toby and Huff, the eccentric old tutor of my little brothers.

"You may divide up responsibilities in your household as you see fit," the admiral said to the emperor. "You will be permitted to go on outings—supervised, of course—and you may have visitors. But you are to remember that you are a prisoner here, and as such, you will be guarded continuously." The admiral looked very much like the important British officer he was when he made these caveats. "Look out the window," the admiral added.

Bonaparte frowned and did not comply. "I am well aware, Admiral," he said testily. "I've already taken the trouble to count your charming sentries. *Cent vingt-cinq*—one hundred twenty-five, with bright, shiny bayonets."

I looked outside the window and saw a long row of red-coated sentries. I hadn't seen them when I'd entered the Pavilion. They must have been positioned at the edge of the woods and moved in closer within the past several minutes.

"You need never inquire as to how far you may safely venture forth on St. Helena," the admiral said to him. "Note the position of the sentries, and you will know your limits. During the daylight hours you may go for a ride, but my orderlies will accompany you."

"*Naturellement*," the emperor grumbled.

"At nine o'clock each evening the cordon of sentries will form a ring around the Pavilion. You may walk in the garden if you wish. But at the stroke of eleven you will not be permitted to so much as step off the veranda. I might add that all roads are patrolled, night and day. Over twenty-two hundred soldiers in all. And lest you think of escaping by sea, be assured that two well-armed brigs stand watch over the coast."

The emperor yawned. "Escape? Really, Admiral, you flatter me. I am a fair swimmer, but surely you know that the nearest land is over nineteen hundred *kilomètres* away. I'm not sure they would welcome me in Africa, in any case, since I once put down a Negro revolution in Haiti!"

The admiral was not amused. "Elba was an island too, sir."

I had a dim recollection that the emperor had once before been sentenced to exile—on the island of Elba in the Mediterranean. Somehow, he'd escaped. He certainly would have been much better off staying there, since it was no doubt a nicer place than St. Helena. I supposed that exiling him to St. Helena was a last-ditch attempt to stow him in a place so remote, he'd have little chance of ever escaping again.

"I made myself a little kingdom when I was captive there," Bonaparte said. Then, with mock petulance: "It was too small. I outgrew it."

"And your escape cost Europe sixty thousand of its young men," the admiral said bitterly, his whiskers bristling. "What right had you to trouble the world again with your ambitions?"

Bonaparte stood up and stalked around the room like a lion in a cage. "It was the will of the French people that I return! What right had Britain to choose for them their leaders? Louis XVIII was inflicted upon France by her enemies. Let the Bourbon kings rule England if they like! The French drink wine. They have no taste for Bourbon!"

The emperor paced rapidly up and down, as if he might wear a ravine into the floorboards. He tugged nervously at his sleeves as he walked. He turned to the admiral. "A few hundred men returned with me from Elba—a few hundred, no more. Had the people not welcomed my return, they would have crushed us like insects when we marched into the cities. Like insects! But, instead, from Paris to Provence, they laid down their arms—laid down the arms that their petty leaders had bade them use against me!"

The emperor crossed his arms and sat down. Then he seemed to reach way back into the depths of his memory and dust off some distant recollection. His eyes glazed over, and he was lost in a reverie.

"We marched into Paris," Bonaparte said softly. "Some of my men feared a hostile reception. I know the French. I did not fear. The people thronged about me, cheering, throwing garlands at my feet. Women, young and old, wept for joy. At long last their emperor had returned to salvage France's glory! I reveled in my victory. Until . . . until I saw the battalion of soldiers marching toward me. They were once my men, but now these grizzled veterans belonged to France's puppet-king and they had been sent by him to destroy me!

"We were greatly outnumbered, but my men wished to engage them, taking the offense before we were attacked. But I said, 'No. Wait. These men are Frenchmen still.' Alone and unarmed, I approached them. One old veteran aimed his musket straight at my heart. I ordered my men to hold their fire. I walked toward the veteran till the tip of his bayonet grazed my uniform. 'What! You old rascal,' I said to him. 'Would you fire on your emperor?'

"The man lowered his musket and handed it to me with great solemnity. He said, *'Regarde, Majesté. C'est vide!'*

"I looked down the muzzle. It was empty, just as he'd said. The old man wept and fell to his knees before me and pleaded for my forgiveness. I helped the poor fellow to his feet. 'Rise, sir,' I told him. 'I see by your battle scars that you have fought many times for France. You need never kneel in shame on her soil.'"

The emperor was no longer remembering the past now. He was in it.

"Then I turned to the rest of the battalion and proclaimed, 'Soldiers! In my exile I heard your voice. I have come back in spite of all the obstacles and all the dangers. Your general, called to the throne by the choice of the people and raised on your shields, is restored to you. Come and join him! Come and range yourselves under the flag of your leader. He has no existence except in your existence; he has no rights except your rights and those of the people. His interests, his honor, his glory are none other than your interests, your honor, your glory.

Victory will march at a quickstep. The eagle and tricolor shall fly from steeple to steeple to the towers of Notre Dame! Then you can show your scars without dishonor; then you can pride yourselves on what you have accomplished. You will be the liberators of the fatherland! In your old age, surrounded and admired by your fellow citizens, you will be able to say with pride, "I too was part of the grand army that entered twice within the walls of Vienna, within those of Rome, of Berlin, of Madrid, of Moscow and which cleansed Paris of the pollution that treason and the presence of the enemy had left in it!"'

"I stepped back and waited to see what the soldiers would do. I did not have to wait long. 'Long live the emperor!' they cried by the thousand. Then a great cheer went up among them, and they waved their muskets in the air. They would have raised me up upon their shoulders in joy and triumph had their respect for my position not prohibited it. Mounting my horse, I took my place at the head of my new army and led them on to the center of Paris. They sang 'La Marseillaise' as they marched. 'La Marseillaise'! That song had once been the greatest general of the Revolution. Now it was the anthem of my triumphant return to France!"

The emperor half sung, half spoke in a rough

but passionate voice the stirring words that had inspired millions of Frenchmen to take up arms and fight for their freedom: *"Allons, enfants de la patrie, le jour de gloire est arrivé! . . . Aux armes, citoyens! Formez vos bataillons! Marchons! Marchons! Qu'un sang impur abreuve nos sillons!"*

Exhausted, the emperor leaned back in the chair. Admiral Cockburn was clearly impressed by Bonaparte's performance—almost awed by it, really.

"Is there anything further you wish to say to me, Admiral?" Bonaparte said suddenly.

Cockburn was caught off-guard by the question. He stared blankly at Bonaparte at first, then quickly recovered his dignity. "No. Not at present."

"Bon," the emperor said. He called out: "Gourgaud! Show the admiral to the door."

Gourgaud entered the room so quickly, I was convinced he'd been listening at the keyhole. He led the admiral away.

Admiral Cockburn may have been impressed by the emperor's lengthy dramatic soliloquy, but I was not. All that talk of war, victory, and glory! What a waste of words! I'd heard enough of such things from my father when he reminisced again and again about his glory days in His Majesty's Navy. My brothers always listened, enraptured, when my father told his fiery tales of battle at sea. Naturally enough, as he related them, my father was the hero of every engagement, single-handedly saving the day for king and country. I always found a way to absent myself whenever I sensed my father was about to launch into another of his battle tales. War stories were for old men and little boys. And war was for fools. If Napoleon Bonaparte was the world's greatest general, that only made him the world's biggest fool. What had he ever done in his life but shout orders and lead charges? It was clear to me that the man had far less concern for the greater glory of France than for the greater glory of Bonaparte.

The wars that had gone on during my lifetime always seemed so far away—not quite real. I had never felt any personal connection with them. But while I was at Hawthorne, I recall having sometimes been kept awake at night by a terrible wailing—from the girls, such as my good friend Madeline, who'd learned their brothers had been killed at the front. It was a chilling memory.

The emperor looked at me and raised an eyebrow quizzically. He must have sensed I was unmoved by his tales of glory, because he said, "You appear to be suffering from boredom. *Sans doute,* mademoiselle knows too little of war."

"No, sir," I replied. "Too much."

I immediately regretted my comment, but it was too late to take it back. The emperor's face and left thigh muscles twitched. By now I was quick to recognize the signs of anger in him. I braced for the explosion.

But then, to my surprise, the emperor appeared to swallow his anger. His rage was so enormous that, in fact, it was really more like watching a cobra swallow an elephant. He took a deep breath, and finally, his anger was under control.

"You may leave now, mademoiselle," he said.

I was halfway out the door when he called me. "One moment, mademoiselle," he said quietly.

I suspected that he'd changed his mind and decided to reprimand me after all. But I faced him unflinchingly. "Yes, sir?"

A dark cloud of memory and regret seemed to cast a shadow over his features. I would have given a great deal to know what he was thinking just then. The cloud lifted slightly.

"*Touché,* Betsy," he said.

Chapter 5

It was early afternoon the next day when I began to hear unpleasant rumors that my mother wanted me for a sewing lesson. I knew how to stitch a hem, of course. And I suppose in a pinch I could mend a loose button. That, in my opinion, was quite sufficient. But my mother had other notions—not the least of which was the abiding conviction that all "proper young ladies" should be proficient at lace embroidery. Silly stitched flowers and such. Not at all aspiring to proper young ladyhood, I knew it was my moment to disappear, before Mother and her sewing accouterments could catch up with me.

Fortunately, the stable was deserted. I determined Belle's leg had healed nicely and I could chance riding her. The heady odor of new hay filled my nostrils, bracing me like a tonic.

We burst out of the stable at a canter. The trees went by in a chartreuse blur. A cool wind cut sharply against my teeth, sending thrills up and down my spine. It had been a long time—too long— since I'd ridden Belle, but she answered my every move like we'd never been apart. Like we were one headstrong, wild creature, she and I together.

I glanced behind me. No one in sight. I slowed Belle for an instant to pull my dress up out of the way so I could switch from sidesaddle to astride, as I always did as soon as I was out of public view. Whatever fool determined that ladies should ride sidesaddle? The same one who blessed us with embroidery, no doubt!

"Mademoiselle!" a voice suddenly called out to me; I knew it well. *Blast—caught!* I pulled Belle up short, but I did not turn around. "Or maybe I should call you, 'monsieur,'" Bonaparte added slyly. He and the British guard sent to chaperone him on his outing galloped up to me from out of nowhere. I was suddenly very aware that my calves were showing. The emperor glanced at me sardonically, taking in the sight. Abruptly, I switched my position back to sidesaddle.

"Good afternoon, sir," I said. My cheeks felt warm.

"Don't worry," Bonaparte said. "I will not tell on you. If I tell on you, you shall tell on me."

"Tell on you? About what, pray?" I said. "What have you done?"

"Nothing. Yet," Bonaparte replied, smiling. "But I always think of the future. That is how I got to be emperor, you know."

I patted Belle idly on the neck and contemplated how I might best irritate him.

"I thought you got your empire by making wars against innocent people," I answered. "You said as much yourself."

His British guard looked quite ill at ease, as if his boots were pinching his toes—or he was afraid that Bonaparte might cuff me. But the emperor just laughed.

"Not making wars, mademoiselle," he replied. "Winning them!"

I decided not to remind him that the emperor's winning streak had recently come to an abrupt end.

"Shall you join me on my little excursion?" Bonaparte said, nodding toward his horse. "You mother shan't object, I think. Even the wealthiest young lady in Paris can't claim an English officer as her personal chaperone."

"Well . . . er . . ." I hesitated, struggling to determine just what precisely a proper young lady would do in circumstances such as this, for I was bent on doing the opposite.

"Come, now, Mademoiselle Betsy," Bonaparte scolded and cajoled me. "Captain Poppleton won't mind, will you, Captain?" The guard nodded his head vigorously and sputtered something about "regulations," but the emperor interrupted.

"You see?" said Bonaparte. "Captain Poppleton has no objection. There's a fine officer, without a doubt. Now, what do you say, mademoiselle?"

"I say . . ."

"Yes?"

"I say it's not for me to say."

Bonaparte clicked his tongue and made a *tsk-tsk* sound like a strange bird. "Oh, mademoiselle," he said with exaggerated disappointment. "*Très triste.* I had you pegged as a girl with—how do you British say?—skunk."

"Spunk!" I corrected him. "It's not 'skunk.' Skunk is an animal that makes a bad smell."

"Ah, *oui!*" Bonaparte said. "Of course. My English is not so very good. *Je le regrette.* Please forgive me, mademoiselle."

Finally!—an admission about his atrocious

English. But did he really believe it? I couldn't tell. It was impossible to know when this man was serious! Perhaps, I thought, that was the real secret of his success.

"So," Bonaparte said, tipping his broad-brimmed hat at me, "it is spunk that you haven't got. *Merci. Au revoir*, mademoiselle," and he turned his horse to go.

Poppleton shook his head and followed.

The emperor and Poppleton rode away from me at a leisurely pace. I sat there for a moment on Belle, feeling rather stupid and doughy, like unbaked dinner rolls. Feeling as though, for once, the emperor had gotten the better of me. Finally, I couldn't stand it any longer.

"Wait! *Attendez*, monsieur!" I called out.

Bonaparte turned around slowly in his saddle, as if to pretend he hadn't expected me to change my mind. "You wish something, mademoiselle?"

I gave Belle a gentle tug on the reins to bring us alongside the black charger. "I have decided to go with you," I announced. "Since I am going your way anyway."

"I see. And exactly where were you headed . . . 'anyway'?" Bonaparte asked, stifling a smile.

I ignored his question. I would not let him gloat.

As we rode, Bonaparte and I feigned amiability, chatting about nothing in particular—the prospects for rain, the state of everyone's health. The sorts of things adults discuss when they don't want anyone to know what they're really thinking.

We started at a walk, proceeded to a trot, then progressed to a canter. I began to get the idea that his small talk was only intended to distract me. What the emperor really wanted was a horse race.

In the midst of a debate about his theory that my father's yams caused indigestion, Bonaparte suddenly nudged his horse in the sides with his silver spurs. And he was off!—galloping away at a furious pace. I could hear his merry laughter on the breeze, and I was determined that he should not win. I followed.

Belle kept apace with the charger, though I worried if her game leg would hold. Poor Captain Poppleton, astride a tired old nag and bouncing along with his musket and rusty canteen, was falling far behind us. Soon he was a dot in the distance—tearing his hair in frustration, no doubt.

Before long I passed the emperor, who muttered French oaths under his breath. Then I drew up on the reins and waited for him by the mouth of a cave. I hadn't intended to come to this spot, but it was a path Belle and I had followed so many times that instinct must have guided me here.

"You are quite a horsewoman, Betsy," Bonaparte said as he came upon me, breathless. He found me yawning, standing calmly beside Belle, as if I'd been waiting for him for an eternity. "I could have used more like you at Acre."

Acre? I had never heard of the place, but I assumed it was some sort of battle of his that hadn't gone so well for him.

"Merci." I acknowledged his compliment without making a fuss over it.

"I would like to race Hope someday. At the English races. That has always been my dream. But I don't think your king would approve."

I smiled at his attempt at wit, then nodded toward his charger. "Hope. That's his name?"

"Ah, *oui.*"

"He doesn't have the shape for it," I said, scrutinizing the horse with my practiced eye. "That's no racer. He's a warhorse. All those big, heavy bones—"

"Nonsense!" the emperor replied. "Surely you know I let you win."

Of course I knew this to be untrue, but I let it pass.

Bonaparte dismounted and stretched with a

grimace. I suppose it had been a while since he last rode in battle, and he was out of practice. He glanced in the general direction of the Briars.

"It appears Captain Poppleton is absent without leave," Bonaparte said, not without amusement. "Ah," he said with a sigh, "how much simpler it all would be if I had Roberaud with me now."

"Is he a friend of yours?"

"*Un ami?*" Bonaparte mused. "Not really. We are too much the same. He is my double."

"Double?"

The emperor nodded, as if that should make everything crystal clear. But I kept staring at him, so he sighed impatiently and explained: "Let's say the Emperor Napoleon is about to go someplace where he would be in more than the usual danger. Oh, not the battlefield. Nothing so tame as that. Say, London Bridge, *par exemple*. Or a visit to his wife's mother! The emperor stays home and eats licorice and sends Roberaud in his place." Bonaparte shrugged. "No one is the wiser."

"Then, he resembles you?"

"He could be my twin," the emperor replied, tethering our horses to a tree. "Now, let us examine the events of today," he continued. "If Roberaud were here, I could have left him back at the Pavilion with Poppleton and the others. And then I could have sneaked out like a tomcat to go for my ride on Hope. As far as I like, without a chaperone. No one would know I was gone. *C'est bon?*"

"Where is Monsieur Roberaud now?" I asked.

Bonaparte squinted, as if trying to remember something. "I heard he escaped when I was captured at Waterloo. If I know Roberaud, he's sitting under the apple trees in the countryside of *la belle* France. Normandy, perhaps. Waiting for his orders. Wooing the ladies. He takes after me that way, you know."

The emperor fell silent. He seemed a trifle sad—as if he longed to sit under the apple trees again himself but knew he never would.

"Would you like to see my cave?" I offered. I don't know what made me suggest it. I had never brought anyone here before.

"Hmmm?" I seemed to have startled him from a reverie.

"Follow me," I said, and led the way. He raised no objection.

Though it was still daylight, the cave was dark, even near the entrance. That was one of the reasons I had chosen it as my occasional refuge to begin with. No one would suspect it held anything of interest.

I crouched and edged my way through the passageway. The ceiling was low and hard, lethal limestone spikes jutted from it, formed by the minerals dripping from the ceiling over the centuries.

"Watch out for your head," I warned the emperor as he followed me.

"Advice that King Louis would have done well to take," Bonaparte said cheerfully. I suppose he was referring to the king who'd gotten his head chopped off by the guillotine during the French Revolution. I thought his joke in very poor taste.

I'd grown several inches taller since my last visit here, but I found this posed no problem. And Bonaparte was an unusually small man, hardly larger than I—in height, that is to say, not in girth. So he had only to bend a bit and follow me through the passageway. But the cave smelled dank and foul, like a thousand wet hounds that hadn't enough sense to come in from the rain. A bone-chewing chill emanated from its every nook and cranny, like a blast of retribution from an angry deity. This was not lost on the emperor.

"What do you keep in this godforsaken place, mademoiselle?" he inquired, shuddering. "Roquefort cheese? Relations who have gone *fou*?"

I knew enough French to know that *fou* meant

"insane." My relatives are all quite normal, thank you. But I should think an investigation of the emperor's family tree would prove more fruitful.

Suddenly, a vast and terrible blackness burst from the bowels of the cave like a messenger of death. The extraordinary sound accompanying it was as if an entire library of books had suddenly emptied itself of its pages from a tremendous height. The black, leathery "pages" brushed my cheeks in a very unwelcome caress, and my hair was disarranged by a thousand unseen hands.

"Argh!" the emperor called out, startled. He was probably having an experience similar to mine, but it was too dark for me to see him clearly.

"Are—are you all right, sir?" I asked him. Even in the dimness, I detected his arms swinging wildly about his head like blades on a windmill.

Then, in a moment, it was over.

"Flying rats!" he said contemptuously. "Just like in Egypt. I'd rather fight a thousand Mameluke armies!"

"The bats won't hurt you," I said casually. "We just startled them. They were sleeping."

"I trust they will accept our apologies," the emperor said facetiously. He was quiet for a moment and stood motionless. I could hear the slow *drip . . . drip . . . drip* of the limestone spikes being formed in the cave, a fraction of an inch at a time; the slow drip of time. Bonaparte said nothing and contemplated, as if time were something in endless supply. And to him, now, here a prisoner, I suppose it was. It was as if he were replaying the whole bat episode in his mind, as a general does after a battle to see what went right and what wrong. At last he spoke to me. His tone was at once puzzled and amazed.

"You did not scream."

"You did," I replied.

Chapter 6

I had plenty of time to savor my victory as we wended our way along the narrow pathways of the cavern. I led the way. It gave me a good deal of pleasure to know that this man, who'd led a million men to their deaths on the field of battle, was now reduced to following me, a mere girl of fourteen years. A fitting fate for a man who had brought so much misery upon the world. Who never did anything of value, nor gave a thought to anyone but himself.

Perhaps if he had gone to a strict English school like mine he'd have turned out differently. First, the teacher would rap the young Napoleon's knuckles, a bit, with the ruler. Bonaparte would bawl like a brat, no doubt. For my part, I never cry when I get it. Next, the headmaster would administer the paddle to his *derrière*—as the French politely call the "bottom"—until it was as purple as a plum pudding. *Now, Master Bonaparte*, he'd lecture him. *You have been a very obstinate little boy. You shall go and sit in the corner and ruminate about what you've done.* Oh, yes—he'll be sitting in this corner of the world for a long, long time. . . .

"Mademoiselle Betsy," the emperor said, interrupting my delicious speculation. "Your cave is *très charmante*—very charming—but I think I have seen enough, and it is getting late. Shall we retreat? I would not want to give our Captain Poppleton the apoplexy."

I ignored him for a few steps more—down a steep incline—and then we arrived at our destination. I reached in the crevice, and the stickiness of a spider's web enveloped my hand. Was the lamp still there? Ah, yes! And with fresh oil and flints, to boot. Huff must have been there recently. I struck a flint against a striker and lit the wick.

Holding the lamp aloft, I turned to face the emperor in time to see the astonished look on his face. You see, it was not just the lamp that caught him by surprise. It was the laboratory.

It had not changed much since I'd been here last. Oh, perhaps there were a few more glass flasks and beakers, filled with liquids every color of the rainbow. The book collection still covered both sides of the cavern walls from floor to ceiling. There were books and papers, all shapes and sizes, written in every tongue known to man. Some had been there so long, they were encrusted with green limestone drippings.

The animals were just the same as they'd been— no surprise, since they were all dead and stuffed. The hungry lioness sank her fangs into the graceful neck of the gazelle, frozen in an eternal embrace of death. The mangy hyena cackled silently, and the gorilla stood boldly, baring his teeth and pounding his chest to proclaim his dominion.

The mahogany worktable looked smaller than I recalled. But perhaps since I was bigger now it just seemed that way. A collection of creatures, recently slaughtered, lay on a blood-spattered white sheet on the table. I moved the lamp closer for a better look. The emperor peeked over my shoulder. On the table were detailed anatomical drawings—of what sort of creature, I knew not—done by a steady hand. And nearby a bullfrog was nailed to the sheet with a silver stake through its heart. A set of small pins fixed the skin back, exposing muscles and parts that most people, given a choice, prefer to keep out of public view. I saw Bonaparte wince.

How odd, I thought. *With all the gore he must have seen on the battlefield, he can't stand the sight of blood!*

Bonaparte turned to face me. "This workshop belongs to you?" he said, incredulous.

"Oh, no," I replied. "Of course not. These are Huff's occupations. I just come here when I want to get away from things."

"Huff?"

"My brothers' tutor. He's a little—well, some people think he's rather . . . eccentric."

The emperor ran his hand against the grain of the hyena's fur, kicking up a cloud of dust. "I can't imagine why," Bonaparte said wryly.

I gave him a disapproving look.

"What is he up to here?" the emperor asked.

"Experiments. He's a brilliant scientist," I said, feeling somewhat defensive. "People just don't . . . understand him."

"Ah . . . ," Bonaparte said. "Just as they don't understand Mademoiselle Betsy?"

I was taken aback by his insight. But I tried not to show it.

"Quite so," I said. "Of course, not for the same reasons," I added quickly.

Bonaparte took off his hat—a white, broad-brimmed islander's hat that had been a "welcome" present from Toby—and swept off a rickety chair with it. Then he sat down, put his chin in his delicate hand, and looked at me curiously.

"They do not understand you because you have the gazelle's *liberté* in your soul. But now you are trapped in a pose—as this stuffed creature here." He pointed to the gazelle, frozen in its moment of utter helplessness.

In spite of myself, he had captured my attention, and I didn't say a word. Encouraged, he went on: "Trapped. The role they have written for you does not suit you—like a good actress in a very bad play. You dream of doing great things, but no one expects it of you. Your heart aches to break free—and write your own destiny on the wind. You are not taken seriously. You want to be taken seriously. And someday they will see what they have missed in you—you will make them see. And they will be sorry."

He studied me.

"Ah, with Betsy's jaw dropped open like that, she resembles even more our unfortunate gazelle."

Yes, I confess I was astounded by Bonaparte's analysis. I must have looked very ridiculous, standing there with my mouth gaping open. How could this man, who'd met me only a few days prior, know my feelings so well? It was as if he were one of the girls I'd gossiped with in the darkness of the bunk room after curfew at Hawthorne. *Perhaps Toby has been talking about me,* I speculated, annoyed. *I'll have to have a long talk with Toby. . . .*

"And now mademoiselle is wondering how I could see into her soul, *n'est-ce pas?*" Bonaparte said.

I stared at him. Unfortunately, he could tell by the look on my face that he'd guessed correctly, again.

"You see, mademoiselle, you and I are very much alike."

"What?!" I began angrily. "How can you say—"

"Now, now," the emperor interrupted soothingly. "Hold your fire. When I spoke of your feelings, I merely spoke of my own—when I was your age. You and I are as much the same on the inside as Roberaud and I are on the exterior. And kindred spirits can always recognize one another."

The emperor had a self-satisfied smile on his face that irritated me like an overstarched petticoat.

"What could you and I possibly have in common?" I demanded.

"*Beaucoup!* A great deal. Born in the middle of a large *famille*—though in my case, there were eight *enfants*—I knew when I drew my first breath that I was unlike the others. I struggled to find myself, but there was no niche for me. Then I was sent away to school, far away from everyone known to me—just as you were, mademoiselle. I attended the military academy at Brienne. I did not play by the rules. Like someone else I know," he said slyly. "I was lonely. An outsider. Did not 'fit in,' as the English say."

"Outsider?" What on earth did the man mean?

"I was not French, you know."

Bonaparte? France's greatest "hero"? Not French? Impossible!

He saw my skeptical look and added, "*C'est vrai*, mademoiselle. Quite true. I am Corsican. Born 'Buonaparte.' On a little island that was passed back and forth between France and Italy like a baton. At the academy, shunned for my strange accent and foreign ways. And my . . . er . . . diminutive stature. No one expected I would ever accomplish anything. Little Napoleon do anything of consequence? *Jamais!* But I was determined to prove them wrong. And that would take some time. I ended my glorious career as a scholar forty-second—in a class of fifty-one."

Ninth from the bottom? Even I had done better than that! Well, except my first term, of course.

Still, from this moment forth, I found it increasingly difficult to view Bonaparte as a strange being from another cosmos.

Just then we heard the sound of footsteps approaching. Bonaparte swung around in a flash, hand on his sword. It seems his old warrior's instincts were still alive.

It took a few moments for the intruder to come into the lamplight, but I knew him instantly by his hesitant, arthritic gait.

Chapter 7

"Huff!"

"Betsy? Can it be? Betsy? Is that you, my dear child?" Huff said, squinting in the dimness. He looked much the same as when I had seen him last—still the peculiar red fez on his head, with tassel dangling, still the long white robe like an Arabian prince. His ragged beard was now completely gray, though, and almost reached his navel.

He shuffled toward me, extending his long, bony arms. "Oh, my dear child! How you have grown!" Huff embraced me, and I daresay he shed a tear or two. "Let me look at you."

He stepped backward, and it was then that he noticed I was not alone, for Bonaparte had been lurking, sword aready, in the shadows. Oddly, it seemed the emperor had been intent on defending me, should the need arise.

"Have I . . . interrupted you, my dear?" Huff said, embarrassed. "I will go, of course. . . ." And he turned to leave. I was puzzled at first by his unease. And then it dawned on me: He thought he'd interrupted a romantic tryst!

I couldn't contain a laugh. "No, no!" I said, almost choking with laughter. "Please don't go. It's nothing like that. He's just a . . ."

Bonaparte listened expectantly, waiting to see what word I'd supply to describe him, I suppose. But I was at a loss.

"Acquaintance," Bonaparte supplied in my behalf. "Of the most respectful kind."

"Ah," Huff said, as if that made everything clear. Apparently, his eyesight was none too good. He clearly did not recognize the emperor.

"I hope you don't mind my bringing him here," I said to the old tutor. "We didn't mean to give you a start."

"Quite all right," Huff said, tugging at his beard. "I can use the company. You look to be an officer, young man. Betsy, you've done well for yourself, my dear." He clapped Bonaparte feebly on the back. It was clear the emperor was not accustomed to such familiarities, but he did not protest.

"Yes," Bonaparte said, amused. "An officer, indeed."

"Well, that's a most commendable profession," Huff said, lowering himself slowly into a chair. "Where are you stationed?"

Bonaparte seemed to be enjoying the charade. "St. Helena," he said. "My orders are that I shall be assigned here . . . indefinitely."

"Marvelous! Then we shall be seeing a lot of you," Huff replied, peering through a lens at an insect specimen pinned to the table. Huff scribbled a few notes with a quill and stood up with agonizing slowness. He extended a veiny, arthritic hand to the emperor. "What is your name, young man?"

Bonaparte said nothing but gave the old man his hand. I wanted to break the news to Huff as gently as possible. But there was no time for shilly-shallying.

"This is Emperor Napoleon Bonaparte of France," I said.

To my astonishment, Huff grabbed on to the seat of his chair and lowered himself painfully to one knee. He doffed his hat and bowed his head. The lamplight danced off his shiny bald spot.

"Forgive me, Your Majesty," Huff said quietly.

Bonaparte seemed as mystified as I by the old man's actions, but he was clearly pleased. For my part, I was afraid Huff would fall and break his hip.

"Huff!" I protested, taking him by the arm. "No need to do that. Please stand up, my friend. He's just a prisoner now."

Bonaparte's eyes flashed fire at me.

Huff raised his bowed head and stared at me with what can only be described as horror.

"Just a prisoner?!" Huff said. I'd never known him to look so angry. He pounded the seat of the chair, albeit weakly. "Young lady, it seems they have not taught you properly in your fancy school!"

"Now, now, old man," Bonaparte said, helping Huff to his feet. I was surprised by the tenderness the emperor showed him. He could not have been more gentle had he been assisting his own mother. "No need to kneel to me. I can see you are a man of accomplishment yourself." He glanced around the room. "Why secrete it away here?"

"Thank you, Your Majesty," Huff said as he settled back into his chair, wheezing. "When I had my laboratory at the Briars, one of my experiments with electricity—I shall show it to you if you like, sir—caused some commotion—"

"He blew up the cellar," I amplified.

"—and I was banished forever from doing my work there," Huff continued. "And when the magistrate got wind of it, anyplace else on St. Helena was forbidden to me as well. Betsy told me of this cave, where she went when in search of solitude. She offered it to me so I could continue my experiments in secrecy."

The emperor nodded solemnly, as if to promise he would keep the old man's secret. Huff fixed me where I stood with his cloudy blue eyes. I sensed I was about to receive a lecture.

"Now, young lady, let me attempt to rectify the deficiencies in your education. The man who stands before you is a political and military genius. Now, don't look at me that way, Betsy. Take heed. Bonaparte is the greatest conqueror of our time! The victor at forty battles. Lord and master to seventy million souls."

"Eighty," the emperor corrected him politely.

"The rightful successor to Alexander the Great!" Huff continued with a flourish. He nearly toppled from his chair, and the emperor reached out to support him.

"Ah," I said sarcastically. "You mean he was a dictator."

"Dictator?" Huff said. "Do you call the president of the United States a dictator?"

"Don't tell me he was president, too," I remarked, pretending to yawn.

"None of your nonsense, young lady," Huff scolded me. "Bonaparte was elected as surely as any American president—by a vote of the people. The constitution that first brought him to power in France was approved by a vote of three million—to only twelve hundred against!"

"I must be truthful," Bonaparte said. "You are not correct, monsieur."

Huff and I looked at him questioningly.

"It was fifteen hundred against," Bonaparte said, smiling. "And how I would have liked to have conversed with them."

Huff chuckled.

"And when they made him first consul for life, more than half a million more people gave him their votes," the old man added.

"But now there were ten thousand against," Bonaparte interjected. "They did not mind the company of Napoleon for a little while, but for some, a lifetime seemed *excessif*. As old Docteur Franklin used to say in his *Poor Richard's Almanac*: 'Fish and visitors stink after three days.'"

I was not impressed. I had already known of Bonaparte's military exploits. Knowing he was elected to the post of "professional murderer" did nothing to increase my admiration for him.

"You seem quite interested in my life, monsieur," Bonaparte said to Huff.

"I am half French," Huff replied. "My mother's side."

"Ah," said Bonaparte playfully. "I suppose that's why you knelt only on one knee."

Huff smiled toothlessly at him. "And I am also an admirer of greatness," the old man added.

Bonaparte swept off his hat and nodded in acknowledgment. I wrinkled my nose in disgust.

"It seems mademoiselle does not agree with your assessment," the emperor remarked.

"She is young," Huff said with a sigh. "She will learn." His condescension was an annoyance, at best. Huff turned to me once more. "Napoleon Bonaparte brought the blessings of civilization to all of Europe. A gift of knowledge, justice, and order. Had Wellington not stopped him at the Battle of Waterloo—"

"I should have sent my reserve troops up sooner on the seventeenth," Bonaparte muttered, as if refighting the battle in his brain. He shook his head. "I wish I'd died in Moscow. Till then my fame was undiminished. If only heaven had sent me a bullet in the Kremlin! History would have compared me to Julius Caesar!"

"If those fools hadn't stopped him at Waterloo," Huff said again, "he would have gone on to unite the globe, cleaning out the cobwebs of ignorance and injustice from every nation on earth!"

Bonaparte seemed well pleased with Huff's summation and added nothing to it. As for me, I merely shrugged.

"Look here," Huff said to me, standing up with difficulty. He took my hand and led me to an old trunk. Huff struggled to release the catch on a chain around his neck. But his hands did not work too well for such a delicate operation.

"Allow me," the emperor said, undoing the catch. A key dangled from the chain, and with a trembling hand, Huff used it to open the trunk.

Inside was a large flat rock with strange letters carved into its shiny black surface.

"*Mon Dieu!* The Rosetta stone!" Bonaparte exclaimed. "But—how?"

"Not the original, Your Highness," Huff explained. "Just a copy."

I held the lamp over the peculiar rock with its indecipherable message.

"So?" I said.

"This stone," Huff said, taking both my hands in his and staring at me with singular intensity, "will unlock the mysteries of the ages. The secrets of the Pyramids! The riddle of the Sphinx!"

To me, it looked like a rock, not a riddle—with a bunch of boxes and birds and squiggly lines drawn all over it.

"Hold the lamp closer," Huff instructed me. I did as he said. "This stone comes from Egypt, land of the Pharaohs. It is very ancient. Written on it is a single decree in three different tongues. Here we have Greek. Here, the same message in another ancient language, demotic." The emperor and I looked over his shoulder as he pointed. "We scholars know how to read those languages. And here, our great mystery to solve: Egyptian hieroglyphs. We have only to compare the letters of the known languages to the symbols in the unknown one, and we will break the code."

"So?" I said again. "And what does this have to do with the emperor?" Bonaparte surely did not like that I was talking about him as if he weren't present, but for the moment he said nothing.

"The emperor and his men retrieved the original of this precious relic during his military and scientific expedition to the shores of the Nile River in 1799. And, with it, we will be able to open a whole new world of understanding. We shall open a window on the magnificent world of ancient Egypt! How did they mummify their dead? We shall find out. Who built the Pyramids, how, and why? Where are the tombs of the great Pharaohs, with all their golden treasures, to be found?"

"Have you broken the code, as you say, monsieur?" Bonaparte asked.

"I am working on it," Huff replied. "Not yet." He lowered the trunk lid.

"It is treasures like these," Huff said, "that Napoleon Bonaparte lifted from the depths of intellectual darkness into the sunlight of reason. Wherever he has gone, he has left the treasure of enlightenment behind." The old man brushed the dust from his hands, as if he felt he'd had the final word.

I would have responded with an argument, but I really didn't know what to say. I had always admired and respected Huff. He had been one of my few confidants when I was younger. His admiration for Bonaparte took me entirely by surprise, and, I must confess, my respect for Huff's judgment made me feel rather confused. Was it merely because he was half French that he praised the emperor? Or might it just possibly be that Huff was correct about our famous visitor's merits and that I was guilty of misjudging Bonaparte?

Before I could say anything, the emperor removed a pocket watch from his coat and glanced at it. He addressed both of us.

"Marchand is waiting to cut my hair," he said. "So I fear we must be on our way."

He kissed the old man on both cheeks, in the French manner. Rather excessive, I thought, but Huff seemed pleased. I gave Huff a hug in farewell, in the English manner.

As we left the laboratory, Bonaparte took a misstep and bumped into the bookcase. One volume toppled from it. Bonaparte picked up the book, blew the dust from the cover, and recited the title in French. It translated to *Aeronautical Experiments*—by Joseph-Michel and Jacques-Étienne Montgolfier.

"Ah!" Bonaparte said in recognition. "The Montgolfier boys!"

"You knew them?" Huff asked, excited.

"*Mais oui!*" Bonaparte replied. "They wanted to build one of their hot-air balloons for me—for aerial spying on the battlefield. I dismissed them, of course. A good general knows his enemy without viewing the top of his head." The emperor returned the book to the shelf.

We bade *adieu* to Huff, who was staying behind to work on the hieroglyphics, and made our way out of the cave. I couldn't help wondering how feeble old Huff managed the difficult journey through the cave to and from his laboratory every day; but I suppose he had in determination what he lacked in vitality.

Twenty minutes later the emperor and I emerged into the daylight.

"It looks like rain," I said. "We better go back."

"Yes," the Emperor replied. "But, as Docteur Franklin said, it is wise to make haste slowly."

Hope was nuzzling Belle like an amorous suitor.

"Ah," Bonaparte said. "Hope is like myself. He cannot resist a pretty face!"

We mounted up.

There was something I wanted to say to the emperor, now that Huff was no longer with us to take offense at my words.

"You stole the Rosetta stone, didn't you?"

The emperor shrugged. "Borrowed it, one could say."

"My sister Jane says that you have hidden vast treasures. You have stolen from—"

Bonaparte turned on me angrily. "Would you like to know about Napoleon Bonaparte's treasures? Would you, Mademoiselle? Yes, they are vast, but they are not hidden away. The harbors of Antwerp and Flushing, where there is room for the largest fleets in the world. The waterworks I built at Dunkirk, Havre and Nice. The huge docks of Cherbourg, the port of Venice. The high roads from Antwerp to Amsterdam, from Mainz to Metz, and from Bordeaux to Bayonne. The passes over Simplon, La Corniche, and Mont Genèvre, which open the Alps in four directions and excel all the constructions of the Ancient Romans. More treasures? More?"

I looked at him blankly. He continued.

"The re-establishment of the church destroyed by the Revolution. The setting up of new industries, the new Louvre Museum, warehouses, streets, the water supply of Paris. The quays along the river Seine. The revival of weaving mills in Lyons, and building of the Rhine-Rhone canal. More than four hundred sugar factories. The roads from the Pyrenees to the Alps, from Parma to Spezia, and from Savona to Piedmont. The bridges across the Seine, and others in Tours and Lyons. The Napoleon Museum, where, I assure you Mademoiselle, the works of art have been obtained by purchase or peace treaties. These—these are all the treasures of Napoleon and will outlast the centuries!"

For the second time that day I was speechless. Could it be? Could one man—one man—really have been responsible for all those achievements?

We rode the rest of the way back to the Briars in silence.

Chapter 8

"**O**uch! Marchand! Those are scissors, not the guillotine. Take care!"

The emperor patted the spot of blood on his neck where his valet had accidentally nicked him. It was merely a small scratch—I could see that from where I stood—but the emperor ordered, "Get a tourniquet!"

"I am very sorry, Your Majesty," Marchand said, fetching a towel. "But you did not hold still. I warned you."

"You blame me for my own wound?" Bonaparte said in a pique. He turned toward me. "Never let a Frenchman cut your hair, Betsy!"

"I will try to remember that, sir," I said, really having no idea what he was talking about.

Watching a man get his hair cut was not my idea of an exciting way to spend an afternoon. But since I'd returned from school, I had lots of time on my hands and little to do with it. According to my father, my education was now complete. "No girl should stay in school past the age of fourteen" was his motto. When my mother suggested that additional years of schooling might benefit me, my father flew into a rage. "What are we training Betsy for?" he boomed. "Governor-general of India?!"

As always, my mother surrendered.

I can't say I was disappointed at not returning to Hawthorne. And I daresay they would not be disappointed at not seeing me. But I felt I'd only exchanged one prison for another. What on earth was there for a girl to do on this miserable rock? I could dig up yams with the slaves. Learn sewing and other drivel from my mother. Listen to Jane's whining. Or watch the former emperor of France get his hair cut. It was not difficult to choose.

Marchand patted the emperor's neck as delicately as a baby's bottom. "There now, Sire," his valet soothed. "The bleeding has stopped."

"No thanks to you!" the emperor grumbled. He brushed some fine, dark hairs off his shoulders. Marchand handed him a looking glass so he could see the results of his labors. The emperor turned his head from side to side.

"*Petit Tondu*," he said, looking critically at his reflection.

"Sir?" I said, wondering what he meant.

"Little Crop-Head," he translated. "That's what the boys called me at the academy. It was not intended as a compliment."

"They called me 'The Colonies.' When I was at school."

Bonaparte ran his hand through his shorn locks and looked at me quizzically.

"Because I was always in rebellion, as the Americans rebelled against the English," I explained. The emperor smiled and hopped off the chair.

"*Viens.* Come," he said, sweeping out of the room. I did not know where he was leading me, but neither did I particularly care. I followed.

We arrived in another room of the Pavilion. It was rather damp and chilly and filled with unpacked boxes. He had been right to compare it to the Russian winter.

"I will show you my autobiography," Bonaparte said, approaching a large wooden crate filled with straw that was labeled SÈVRES; TUILERIES. He knelt and pulled straw out of the box rapidly, like an eager child unwrapping Christmas presents.

The object he pulled from the box was enveloped in old, yellowing copies of French newspapers. He unwrapped it. It was nothing but a china plate with a picture on it. He showed it to me pridefully.

"I thought you were going to show me your autobiography?" I said.

"Exactement!" Bonaparte said. He lifted some more plates out of the box, leaving such a pile of straw scattered about that I felt I was in a pig barn. "These Sèvres plates from the Tuileries were made for me. They tell the story of my life."

Intrigued, I looked carefully at the first plate.

"Shall you help me to unwrap them?"

I nodded and reached into the box.

"Of course, they are not in correct order of time," he said, unwrapping plates as he spoke. He showed me their pictures.

"Here is the Battle of Austerlitz. The greatest victory of my career! You were four years old at the time, mademoiselle."

"Against whom?" I asked.

"Russia and Austria," he replied. He showed me another plate that depicted rearing horses and soldiers with muskets and cannon. A few men lay on the ground in dramatic poses with red bloodstains on their uniforms. Who would want to eat dinner off of a plate like this? It would give me gas! A likeness of Bonaparte on horseback, his sword raised in the air—thinner and better looking than he is in the flesh—was prominent in the painting. "*Bien sûr,* sometimes the artist exaggerates a trifle," he told me, grinning. "I fought that battle from my carriage!" He chuckled.

I unwrapped two more plates. One showed a lovely, dark-haired woman, her skin creamy white like a dove's breast. She wore a beautiful necklace of sapphires, surrounded by tiny sparkling diamonds. Her smile seemed to hold a secret, like the lady Mona Lisa's in the famous painting by da Vinci.

"Who is she?" I asked the emperor.

A wistful look passed over his features, followed by some long-ago memory of pain.

"My Joséphine," he said quietly, as if fearful of disturbing someone's sleep.

"Is she your wife?"

"Once upon a time." The emperor sighed. "*Ma belle*—sweet and matchless Joséphine. . . ." He rubbed his eyes.

I did not ask him what had happened to her. I feared it might be too painful for him. I did not think I would ever care about offending the emperor's feelings, but it was hard to remain unaffected by the pitiful look on his face.

"We'll open this one," I said, handing him another plate. I hoped the change would cheer him, but I fear I chose unwisely, because when he removed the wrapping, we saw that this was a portrait of another handsome lady, with a charming, blond-haired little boy about my brother Alexander's age.

"My son," Bonaparte said, struggling to keep control of his emotions. "The King of Rome. And his mother, Marie-Louise."

"Where are they now?" I asked him.

"Held prisoner, as I. At Schonbrunn Castle in Austria," the emperor said. He looked long and hard at the plate. He spoke softly, as if to himself. "Will they teach him to hate his father?"

I struggled to think of a comforting thing to say, as I had at family funerals. This time I had somewhat more success. "Perhaps you will see him again," I said hopefully. "And you will teach him the truth about you, yourself."

The emperor nodded, but I could see he was not optimistic. Then I added meaningfully, "As Huff has taught me."

Bonaparte looked up at me slowly. There was a burning light of gratitude in his eyes—and of victory, too. I suppose he had looked similarly at Austerlitz, and I could see why men would follow him—yes, even march to their deaths—for a chance at his approval.

I began to feel uneasy, wondering if I should have a sense of triumph or defeat. Who had won the day? The emperor or I?

Just then we heard footsteps and voices in the other room. It seemed that the admiral had arrived to discuss provisions for the Pavilion with Bertrand, the emperor's grand marshal. An instant later someone else came running into the room in search of the admiral. Whoever it was was clearly beside himself with excitement. Bonaparte and I eavesdropped on the conversation.

"Admiral! Admiral!" the excited man called out, breathless.

"What is it, Captain?" the admiral replied. "What's wrong?"

"Oh, there you are, sir. I've—I've lost the emperor! He has ridden off and escaped! I have looked all over the island for him, but—but he got away from me!"

"He's playing with you, Poppleton," the admiral said calmly. "I'm sure you'll find his horse in the stables. And he'll be eating his supper, happy as a lark. General Napoleon, that is, though likely his horse, too."

The emperor and I looked at each other and giggled like small children. When we regained our composure—which took some time, I confess—we turned our attention back to the task at hand.

Bonaparte removed the last plate from the box and unwrapped it. "Ah!" he said. "My prize!" He showed it to me. There was no picture on this plate, just some words. "The Code Napoleon," he said pridefully. "The plate cannot contain it all. Written here is a summary only."

"A code? Like the one on the Rosetta stone?" I asked.

"No, mademoiselle," he said. "Not that sort of code. These are laws, guaranteeing rights for all citizens. I gave these laws to France. And I would have given them to the rest of the world, also, if your charming General Wellington's army hadn't stopped me."

I struggled to translate the words scripted on the plate: "Indi-individual liberty," I read. "Freedom of—"

"Freedom of work," the emperor said. "Freedom of conscience. Freedom of religion. Equality of all men before the law."

"But—but that sounds like the American Constitution!"

"The Americans stole it from the French," Bonaparte said, smiling. "From our philosophers—Monsieur Rousseau and others. Though the Americans had their little revolution before ours."

Freedom. Rebellion. What a lovely idea. I thought I could be happy living in France.

"Did you write these laws?" I inquired.

"Enough of them," Bonaparte said.

Well, well, I thought. Perhaps he wasn't such a dictator, after all. Perhaps Bonaparte's loss wasn't exactly the world's gain.

I helped him set up his plates on the fireplace mantel. A cold draft blew through the room. The emperor shivered and asked me if I'd have my father send some firewood. I agreed. Then I went home to supper.

It was only a short walk from the Pavilion to the Briars. As I was rounding the corner, someone grabbed me by the arm. I screamed—but was cut short by a hand quickly clapped over my mouth. The moment my eyes showed I had recognized who had detained me, my "gag" was removed.

"Huff! What's the matter?"

"Shhh! Come with me. . . ." the old man said in a whisper, leading me to a secluded place behind a banyan tree. There was an armed sentry standing nearby, charged with keeping an eye on the emperor. I thought he was an extraordinarily handsome fellow.

"Are you quite all right, Miss Balcombe?" the sentry called out to me.

"Er . . . yes, sir!" I replied, surprised that this fine-looking soldier knew who I was. He caught me staring at him, and to my astonishment, he winked at me. Then he tipped his hat and continued on his rounds.

I turned toward the old man. "What is it, Huff?"

"I need your help, my dear," he said.

"Are Willie and Alexander neglecting their studies again? Surely you know I will not be the best influence on them."

"Shhh!" he said again, drawing me closer. Huff wrung his hands nervously and looked around to see if anyone was observing us.

"Why are you whispering?" I said, a bit annoyed.

"The emperor must continue his good work," Huff said with conviction. "Perhaps he shall lead a Muslim rebellion in Arabia! Or finish what Alexander the Great began and conquer Asia

Minor. He must be allowed to bring freedom and science to all mankind!"

"Well, that sounds like a worthy cause," I said lightly, "but that will be difficult, seeing as how he is holed up here."

"I have a plan for his escape!" Huff replied, as simply as if he were noting the weather.

Escape! God's nightgown! It seemed the old man really had lost his mind.

"And you are going to help me," Huff added.

"What? I will do no such thing. Really, Huff, I think you have been sniffing at your chemicals too long." I started to walk away from him.

"Betsy, wait! Betsy! Please," he said, following. "Just let me speak."

I stopped. A fair hearing? I owed the old man that, at least. I spun around to face him and crossed my arms. "Well?" I said impatiently.

Huff put his bony arm around my shoulders. "Think, my dear—just think what it will be like, to be known as the girl who freed the great Napoleon Bonaparte! The girl who enabled the achievements of the Revolution to be spread across the globe!"

"Ridiculous!" I said. "Why—why, can't you see? I'd cause a scandal! A bloody outrage! No one could ever imagine the daughter of William Balcombe capable of such a thing! My family—the whole British Empire—will have a—a—blathering fit!"

Huff lifted my chin with his long fingers and looked straight into my eyes. He nodded slowly. Very slowly.

Hmmm, I thought. So I could stir up a delicious commotion, free the emperor, and save the world in the bargain, eh? Not half bad for a girl who was bored senseless and had failed Miss Bosworth's history lessons at school.

The light dawned.

"I'll do it," I said.

Chapter 9

I arranged to meet Huff at his laboratory the next morning. He would tell me no more about his plans for Bonaparte's liberation until then. But he did make one request—and an odd one, at that. He asked me to bring as many silk dresses as I could find. To beg, borrow, or steal them, if need be. But that whatever I did, I should under no circumstances reveal the purpose to which they'd be put. Of course, I could not have revealed what I did not know in any case.

The next morning after breakfast I went up to my room, pleading a headache. After determining that I was indeed alone, I opened the clothes chest. The musty odor of mildew assaulted my nostrils. Since prissy Jane changed her dresses so many times each day, it was a miracle that the wooden chest stayed shut long enough to acquire such a singularly unpleasant odor. I held my breath and looked through the dresses to see what I could find: the pink one; the floral one with the flounces that I hated so much; the horrid green one Cousin Cassandra had handed down to me. None of my dresses were silk— just cotton, because I did not care about the latest fashion. A girl could run like a horse in cotton. Silk just made me sweat like one. But Jane liked finery and would not run to save her life, so I was pleased to discover that most of her frocks were of the type that began life with the labors of prized Chinese silkworms. Surely, I reasoned, she would not miss a few.

"What are you up to, Betsy?"

As usual, Jane had entered the room with the stealth of a cobra. She stared at me with those cold green eyes shifting slightly from side to side, as if she were looking for a good place to affix her fangs. I stood there holding a bunch of dresses in my arms, praying my wits would not fail me.

"Mother wants these altered," I said, impressed by my own skill at spontaneous invention.

"Why?" Jane said crisply. "What's wrong with them?"

Oh, dear.

"Uh . . . nothing. It's just that . . . er . . . she feels that you've filled out nicely in the bust and that you ought to show it off more." When in doubt, flatter. That always worked on Jane.

"Hmmm," Jane said, pondering.

My, my. A close call. But I couldn't relax, not just yet.

"Mother wants me to show decollétage? That doesn't sound like Mother," Jane mused.

"Well," I said. "I—I was surprised too, at first. But you know how badly she wants you to get married," I said quickly. "The young officers are fond of low necklines. And there are bound to be some parties around Christmas. . . ."

Jane wrinkled her brow. Thinking was always a strain on her, poor dear.

"I see," she said.

At last! I'd convinced her. I barely hid my sigh of relief.

"I'll go down and model them for Mother," she said, reaching to take the dresses from me.

Horrors! Think fast, Betsy!

"Uh, no, you can't do that!" I said, pulling the dresses out of her reach.

"Why not?" Jane replied. "How can she possibly fit them properly without me in them?"

"It's—it's—" *Come on, old girl, you can do it!* "It's going to be a surprise." *Ah!—Betsy's wits come to the rescue again!* "For your birthday. Don't spoil it for Mother. She'll murder me if she finds out I told you."

"Oh," Jane said, utterly convinced. "Don't worry, little sister. I'll keep your secret."

Not bloody likely.

Jane turned to go out the door. I began to relax. Her birthday was so far off, surely I'd think of a way out of this mess by then. God willing. But a second later, Jane leaned in the doorway and faced me again.

"Betsy, are you quite all right? You seem . . . agitated. Like you did that time before the blacksmith pulled your tooth."

"I'm fine, Jane," I said. "I've only been home a few days. I guess I need some time to get . . . used to it."

Jane shrugged and went out the door.

Nearly an hour later, when I was sure she'd left the house on an errand—shopping in town, I believe—I stuffed her silk dresses under the one I was wearing and sneaked out of the Briars.

I found a preoccupied old Huff poring over a calcified book in his laboratory. A large diagram—construction plans for some sort of scientific contraption—was spread out over the worktable, the lamplight casting long shadows over it like huge, dark fingers. The drawing indicated distances and measurements, the dimensions for a basketlike contraption, and an immense bulbous object suspended by strings or wires above it. I suspected that the diagram related in some way to Huff's plans for the emperor.

"Making progress?" I asked him.

"Yaaa!" Startled, the old scholar sprang out of his chair like a man half his age. "For mercy's sake, Betsy! You'll stop an old man's heart!"

"Sorry," I said.

Huff sat back down and pointed to the diagram. "This will carry the emperor to freedom."

Then he referred back to the tome he was reading. I looked over his shoulder. It was the same book the emperor had knocked from the shelf the previous day—the Montgolfier brothers' book of aeronautical experiments. Huff was reading the chapters about construction of a hot-air balloon.

"You mean, the emperor's going to *fly* off St. Helena?" I asked.

"Precisely," Huff said. He looked me up and down. "You've put on weight, my dear. Try to dipense with it. We need you as light as possible for our test flights."

Test flights? You wouldn't get me up in one of those things! As for my supposed tendency toward corpulence, I removed the wad of silk dresses from under my gown and handed them to him.

"Ah!" he said. "Thank you, my dear. I knew I could count on you."

The old man started ripping Jane's dresses into long strips.

"Huff! Those are Jane's! She'll eat me alive!"

"Never mind, my dear," Huff said, continuing his work.

It was not difficult for me to figure out how those dresses would be used. The balloon would be constructed out of them! How would Jane feel to know her dresses were instrumental in the escape of Britain's most famous prisoner? I must say I smiled at the thought.

"Here is a needle and thread," Huff said, handing me a red velvet box. "I need your young eyes and hands."

"What do you want me to do?"

"Sew the pieces back together side by side. Like this," he said, showing me the balloon diagram.

"I'm afraid sewing is not my strong suit. Mother was going to show me—"

"Never mind," Huff said again with a wave of

his hand. "You will get better at it as you go along."

I sighed, threaded the needle, and began sewing, after a fashion. What irony! Who would have thought I'd ever regret not having taken more sewing lessons!

"Ouch!" I pricked my finger. I sucked the metallic-tasting drop of blood from my fingertip. "Wtdsthemprhvtsybtalofths?"

"What? Speak plainly, my girl! Don't talk with your fingers in your mouth."

"I said, what does the emperor have to say about all of this?"

"About escaping in my balloon?" Huff asked. I nodded. "I don't know."

"What! You mean, you haven't told him?"

"There is no need for him to know," the old man explained, "until the very last moment. And it would be inadvisable to tell him before then."

I gave him a puzzled look. He elaborated.

"First of all, there are spies everywhere. And it will be difficult to get the emperor alone to tell him."

Huff was right about that. I thought of Poppleton and the others who guard the emperor. And what about the meddlesome Gourgaud? I could not imagine that any secret would be safe with him—and surely he'd get wind of this one if the emperor knew of it. "In any case," Huff added, "I do not want to give the emperor too much time to think about our plans. As you saw yesterday from his reaction when we spoke of the Montgolfiers, he is not enamored of aeronautics. But he is a man of action and of courage! If we simply present him with the finished product, he will recognize our balloon represents his only hope of freedom—and climb aboard."

"Well, perhaps you are right," I said. "Though I really wish you'd let me tell him."

"No! It must remain a secret!" Huff said, the tassel of his fez vibrating with his excitement. "And there is no time to waste! We must finish the balloon before he is moved to Longwood. When will that be? Have you heard?"

I strained to remember what I'd overheard the admiral say to my parents. "Perhaps a month or two, I think."

"Good!" said Huff, drumming his fingers on the table. "That will give us just enough time." He stood up slowly and paced the dirt floor of the cave. "At Longwood he will be watched more closely. It would be nearly impossible to effect his escape from there. And around the time he's transferred to Longwood—no one knows just when—the new governor will arrive. The emperor's new jailer. I hear Sir Hudson Lowe is not so . . . flexible a man as our Admiral Cockburn."

I wondered what kind of jailer Governor Lowe would be and what sort of life he had in store for the emperor. Huff interrupted my thoughts.

"We shall need more dresses, Betsy. These are not nearly enough. Can you get more?"

I shook my head.

"Not from Jane, anyway. I fooled her once. She won't fall for the same trick again."

"This presents us with difficulties." Huff sighed.

He rubbed his forehead, thinking. Then he seemed to get an idea. He reached in his long, white robes and produced a few guineas—or what we called "guineas," since English coins were so scarce on St. Helena that we all used Spanish reals, Dutch "lion dollars," Venetian ducats, or silver rupees as a substitute.

"Here," he said, handing me the money. "Go into Jamestown. A supply ship came in shortly before you returned to St. Helena. Perhaps it brought bolts of silk for the ladies. There are shops that sell such things, are there not?"

"I suppose so," I said.

"Buy as much as you can."

I put down my sewing and prepared to go.

"And make sure you are not observed," the old man warned.

Chapter 10

Thank heaven I hadn't run into Jane when I was in town that day. My mission was complicated enough. And for the next few weeks I led a double life. By day I visited the emperor—with whom I'd now gained such familiarity that I occasionally called him "Boney"—or sat for my mother's tiresome lessons in the wifely arts. By night I sneaked out of the Briars to build the balloon in Huff's laboratory. There was always the threat of discovery, and time was growing short. Thanks in part to the silks I managed to acquire in Jamestown, the work was proceeding apace.

One evening I was asked to join the emperor and his suite at supper. I suppose this meant that he had taken me into his confidence, because the conversation seemed unguarded despite my presence.

"What do you miss most about home?" the Countess de Montholon, wife of one of Bonaparte's aides, asked the emperor. It did not escape my notice that she appeared to be flirting with him. Her husband didn't seem to mind.

"I will not give the answer you expect, Countess," the emperor replied with a grin. *"C'est le vin."* The wine! There were knowing laughs from the others. "I do not know what the English call the bottled liquid they bring on ships to us here, but in France, it would be emptied out the bilge."

Unlike the others, Gourgaud seemed very troubled at the mention of home. He got up suddenly from the table and faced a wall, pressing his head against it.

"Oh, *liberté*!" he wailed. "Why am I a prisoner!"

"Gourgaud," the emperor said calmly, as if he'd heard this all before. "Sit down and finish your meal. Save your drama for after, when we read Voltaire."

"Your Majesty!" Gourgaud said, turning around to face us. "Did I not save you from that Cossack at Brienne?"

"You are a brave man but amazingly childish,"

the emperor replied. "Now, please join us."

Yes, the emperor was right. Gourgaud was acting rather silly. But I couldn't help feeling sorry for him. On the other hand, nobody else was complaining, why should he?

"What is the matter with all of you?" Gourgaud said, waving his hand from one end of the table to the other. Everyone put their forks down and stared at the agitated man. "Don't—don't you miss your friends, your families? The homes you left behind? You go quietly, as lambs to the slaughter! Have you no feelings?"

I wondered how the emperor would respond to this outburst. Would he order Gourgaud's head in a bucket? I think the others were as fearful as I.

But the only sound was the rustling of the curtains in the evening breeze. No one knew what to say, least of all I. It reminded me of the times my parents were not on the best of terms and we all had to suffer our way through a meal in frigid silence. At last the emperor broke the ice.

"My dear Gourgaud, how glum you look!" Bonaparte said cheerfully. He stood and put his arm around the man's shoulders. "Isn't it true that it is better to be selfish, unfeeling? If you were, you wouldn't worry about the fate of your mother or sister, would you?" The emperor guided the now pliant Gourgaud back to his chair.

"Have a cold rubdown; that will do you good," the emperor advised. He walked back to his place at the head of the table. Bertrand rushed to pull out his chair for him—just in time, like a carefully rehearsed dance. Bonaparte sat. "One must curb one's imagination. Otherwise, one is liable to go mad. I want my friends to cheer me, not make me sadder by pulling long faces."

"I—I will do my best, Sire," Gourgaud said, sniffling.

"There's a good fellow," Bonaparte said.

The emperor picked up his fork. Everyone began eating again. Madame Bertrand rattled on about what the ladies would be wearing in Paris this year. I was relieved the whole unpleasant episode was over. Or so I thought.

"Do you fancy I have no terrible moments?" Bonaparte interrupted, addressing no one in particular. He stared off into space. "At night I wake up and think of what I was—and to what I have come. But I have no regrets. No one but myself can be blamed for my fall! I have been my own greatest enemy."

I was stunned by this admission. And I admired the emperor all the more for making it.

"But, Sire," Gourgaud said obsequiously, "surely the fact that we've been condemned to this horrible place is not your fault. I did not mean to imply—"

"I know you didn't, Gourgaud," Bonaparte said with a sigh. He looked at me. "And, at times, I too dream of escape."

Good heavens! Did he know of Huff's plan?

"Arghh!"

"Mademoiselle Betsy is choking," Bonaparte said to Bertrand, noticing my distress. "Go to her aid! *Vite!*"

Bertrand bounded to my side and slapped me on the back. A piece of fowl had gotten lodged in my throat, and I coughed and coughed like a plague victim.

"Marchand!" the emperor called into the other room. "Bring water!"

There was talk of sending for Dr. O'Meara. After a moment more I coughed up the offending object like a dog who's eaten too much grass.

By this time the emperor himself was at my side. "I am glad you are still with us, mademoiselle," he said, helping me to the settee. "They would have said I'd poisoned you."

Supper concluded, Bonaparte read to us from

Voltaire's play *Candide*—in a rather too passionate manner. Still, he went on so long that some of us—myself included—showed signs of nodding off.

"Madame, you are asleep!" the emperor barked at Bertrand's wife. That perked her up. Soon after, Gourgaud seemed to be falling into a bowl of pink flowers. "Wake up, Gourgaud!" the emperor shouted.

Gourgaud snorted and quickly sat upright. "At your orders, Sire," he mumbled.

After the interminable selection from Voltaire, the emperor asked me to join him at a game of whist. I worried silently that at this rate I'd never get to Huff's cave tonight. So I replied that I would play the card game but could only stay a short while. Countess Montholon and Bertrand joined us at the card table.

As Bertrand dealt the cards, I studied Bonaparte's face. There was no sign that he knew anything of our plans for his escape. There were no raised eyebrows or other signals vying for my attention. No indication that he wished to communicate with me in private. I was satisfied that no one had told him of the balloon and that my secret was safe. But why had he looked at me when he spoke of escape? Was he trying to ask for my help?

I had a good hand. Hearts were trump, and I had lots of them.

"So, Betsy," the emperor said as he picked up the first trick of cards, "what shall you do with yourself now that you are home from school?"

"I haven't really thought about it," I replied. "I don't think my parents want me to think."

"Tant pis," the emperor said, clucking and shaking his head slowly. He played a knave, rearranged his cards, and studied them. "Have you thought of being a soldier?"

"That is not a job for ladies—*or* gentlemen," I said, picking up a trick of my own.

"Women have been known to go to war like soldiers, and then they are brave, susceptible to great excitement, and capable of committing the worst atrocities," the emperor remarked. "I should like to be present if war broke out between the sexes. It would rival the Battle of Austerlitz!"

I giggled.

"I like to hear you laugh, mademoiselle," Bonaparte said, patting my hand. "It is like good French wine."

Countess Montholon looked at me strangely. If I didn't know better, I'd say she was jealous! The thought gave me a peculiar sense of satisfaction.

"Have you ever been in love?" the countess asked the emperor. It seemed to me an impertinent question—especially for a man who'd had two wives. But Bonaparte answered it.

"It takes time to make oneself loved. And even when I had nothing to do, I always felt I had no time to waste. Besides," the emperor added. "I am too old for it."

Was it true that he had never loved anyone? Even I, a mere child, had been able to tell that he'd loved Joséphine. Ah, but he only said that he'd never "made himself" loved! Not that he had never loved anyone.

I felt very uncomfortable being present for the countess's flirtation with him. She looked at him through heavy-lidded eyes.

"Some men of forty-six," she said huskily, "are still young."

"Some men," the emperor replied sadly, "have not borne my burdens."

It was then that I decided it was time for me to go.

I went home to the Briars, yawned ceremoniously in front of my parents, and went upstairs to bed. Once Jane went to sleep—and the minx stayed up far too late for my convenience, rattling on about some handsome young English ensign named Carstairs who had caught her fancy from afar—I climbed out my window, down the vine, and rode Belle to Huff's cave. By now this had become my regular nightly routine, and the shortage of sleep was beginning to take its toll.

About halfway to the cave a strange sensation came over me. My skin crawled, as if unseen eyes were upon me. And, in a flash, I realized what was amiss. I was being watched! Someone had followed me!

I quickly took a different route to the cave, hoping to keep them off the scent. Riding around several acacias as if traveling through a maze, I hoped to confuse my pursuer. Every now and then, I looked behind me, but I saw nothing. Sometimes I came to a sudden halt—hoping that I'd hear telltale hoofbeats coming up behind me. But my ruse didn't work. Whoever it was had reflexes as quick as my own.

When I finally reached the cave, I waited a long while before entering it. I watched and listened, my heart pounding in my chest like Willie's toy drum. Had I only imagined I was being followed? Perhaps so. Perhaps frayed nerves and lack of sleep were finally catching up with me. *Betsy, old girl, you're letting your imagination run away with you*, I scolded myself.

At last I entered the laboratory. And there it

was: Stretched out on the floor like a gargantuan beached jellyfish, the balloon was nearly finished. And quite a beast it was. The bag must have been thirty feet long, even deflated as it was now. It lacked only a few more silk panels and a gondola to carry the passengers.

"Ah!" Huff said, patting me on the head. "Welcome, my dear! As you can see, we're nearly done. Perhaps a week's labor more, and the balloon shall be ready to fly."

"That's good," I said, taking up my sewing.

"How are the emperor's spirits holding up?" the old man asked.

"Well enough, I think," I replied. "Though I believe he'll be glad at having a chance to escape. Do you think he shall be sorry to leave the others behind?"

Huff shrugged. "You would know that better than I," he said. "But at least he will have an old man for company."

"You—you mean you will be going with him?" I had not thought of this possibility before. I certainly did not like the idea of losing old Huff.

"Of course, my dear. He will need someone to pilot the ship."

We worked in silence for a few moments.

"I shall miss you," I told him.

"And I, you," the old man said. "Don't concern yourself about me, Betsy. I have always wanted to see Paris. I am sure the emperor will take good care of me . . ."

It was about an hour later that I left for the Briars. I was extra cautious in making sure that no one was observing me. And I returned home without further incident.

I scrambled up the vine to the bedroom window. Before I climbed through, I took a deep breath of the damp night air and looked about me. The view was a tonic to my nerves. I listened to the low, soft hum of African spirituals emanating from the slave cabins. Trees swayed in the breeze, as if dancing in time to the music. *How could people living a life of hard labor find anything to sing about?* I wondered. *What inspiration could they draw from soil and yams and sweat?* And yet, somehow, they found it within themselves—a freedom that no one could take away from them. Bonaparte was not the only prisoner on St. Helena. Perhaps that's why he understood me— and Toby, too—so well. In a way, we were all prisoners here. I saw the fires of the soldiers who were camped nearby, burning like yellow stars in the sky. I wondered how the men felt, far from home and family, spending their lives guarding one solitary soul. The emperor was the whole reason for their presence here—the reason for their very existence. Night and day, day in and day out, all attention was focused on him. Was he their prisoner, or they his?

As I considered these questions, lulled by the sound of the music, my hands seemed to loosen their grip on the vine. I was falling!

I slipped and, grabbing on to the rain gutter with one hand, made a mad grab at the vine with the other. Caught it! It took every ounce of strength I had to hang on. I was weary. I looked below me—a long, long drop.

After taking a moment to catch my breath, I climbed through the window. Home at last! I stripped to my nightgown and put a foot in my cozy bed.

Out of the darkness came a voice.

"I know what you're up to."

Chapter 11

"Jane! Uh . . . what are you doing up?" I tried to seem nonchalant, but in fact her words terrified me. And, all at once, I knew with terrible certainty that it was *she* who had followed me to Huff's cave.

"Did you think I would be so stupid that I'd believe your story about Mother needing my silk dresses?"

Yes, Jane, I did think you'd be that stupid.

"I—I don't know what you're talking about," I said.

Jane got up out of bed and faced me. She lit the lamp. I squinted painfully in the sudden brightness.

"It's no use, Betsy," she said, crossing her

arms. "I heard you talking to Huff about that Frenchman. I borrowed Father's horse and followed you into the cave."

"Oh," I said, realizing the game was up.

"How could you—how could you think of doing such a thing?" Jane demanded in her supercilious fashion. "Help him escape? The man is a monster!"

I sat on the edge of my bed and tried to collect my thoughts.

"Shhh! You'll wake the boys," I said. Actually, I was fearful my parents would overhear her. "He's not a monster. He's . . . industrious."

Jane wrinkled her brow. Uh-oh. She was thinking again.

"You're—you're not going to tell Father, are you, Jane?" I asked, fearing the worst.

"Of course I am! What did you expect? That I'd let you set a murderer free?"

"Please don't, Jane! You'll get all of us in trouble. Huff will lose his laboratory, and heaven knows what they'll do to him after that!"

"What do I care for that old lunatic?" Jane said. I could have murdered her for saying that, the little witch! "In fact, I think I'll go wake Father and tell him right now!"

As Jane sashayed out the door, I made a grab at one of her golden ringlets.

"Ow! You horrible creature! Let go!" Jane whined, struggling to get away from me.

"Not until you promise not to tell."

"Ow! Ow! All right—I promise. Now let go!"

I kept my word and released her. She sat down calmly, rubbing the side of her head as if I'd caused her catastrophic injury.

Suddenly, she leaped up and headed for the door. "I crossed my fingers!" Jane said with a cackle. Too late to grab her! She ran into the hallway—the only time I'd ever seen her run.

It was my last chance. Desperate, I ran after her.

"Wait!" I called out.

Fool that she was, Jane stopped abruptly.

"If you tell," I whispered, gritting my teeth, "I'll—I'll tell Father what I saw you doing with Ensign Carstairs!"

It was a wild, desperate guess, but it was my only hope.

Jane's jaw dropped. "It wasn't Carstairs," she said, her shoulders slumping in defeat.

Bull's-eye!

"Didn't think anyone was watching you, did you?" I goaded her.

Jane shook her head sadly. I almost felt sorry for the poor girl. Well, not really.

"James—he's a corporal, you know—promised he'd marry me," Jane said glumly. "When he got his promotion. He promised! But it was all a lie. A vile, vicious, disgusting lie!" Jane flopped down on the hall floor like a small child throwing a temper tantrum and began to sob.

"There, there, Jane," I said, patting her on the shoulder. "He was only a corporal. You can do better than that. You deserve a general at least!"

"I suppose you're right, Betsy," Jane said, wiping her runny nose on her nightdress sleeve. "But—but to think that I—I lowered myself to—!" She dissolved into a whole new cascade of tears.

"There, now, Jane," I said, helping her to her feet. I led Jane by the hand back into our bedroom. "Everything's going to be all right. . . ."

I blew out the lamp. We lay in our beds, holding hands across the gap between them. The sheets heaved with her sobs. I held on to Jane's fingers till she cried herself to sleep, just as she'd held mine long ago, when I was scared of the thunder. Well, she was my sister, after all.

. . .

The next morning, I slipped out unnoticed and went to Huff's cave.

"Jane is on to us," I said, greeting the old man. "She spied on us yesterday."

"Dear, dear," Huff replied worriedly. He shook his head. "She never was my favorite Balcombe child."

"I'm sorry I didn't catch her following me," I said. "It's my fault! I should have been more careful."

"That's all right, my dear," the old man said, patting me on the head. "I'm sure you did your best."

"She's promised not to tell, but I don't trust her. I think we had better speed things up. Can we test the balloon tonight?"

Huff showed me the balloon. The gondola was finished; the balloon, not quite.

"Impossible," he said. "We need a few more days of work on it, at the minimum. Besides . . ." Here, he walked over to the wall where a pear-shaped glass container hung from a nail. There was a red liquid inside, filling about one third of it. Huff peered at it. "The barometer says heavy weather's afoot."

"We'll have to chance it, Huff," I said. "Jane could give us away at any moment."

Huff considered this carefully and concluded I was correct. With a little luck, he supposed he could complete the balloon's cooling vent and other essential parts by this evening, leaving a few extras aside. And perhaps the weather would hold up long enough to suit us. We agreed to meet again that night for a test flight under cover of darkness.

I went back to the Pavilion to keep a close watch on the emperor. I found Willie practicing the piano in the parlor. Or, rather, I should say, he was giving a command performance for the emperor. My brother was amazingly precocious at music, thanks to instruction by the versatile Huff. A prodigy. A young Mozart! I listened to the sonata, enraptured.

The emperor was clearly pleased too. *"Très bien,* William. Very good," Bonaparte said, applauding loudly. *"Formidable!"*

"Not yet!" Willie complained, continuing his playing. "Don't you know you aren't supposed to applaud between movements?"

The emperor took this criticism very well and sat on his hands until Willie was finished.

"Licorice?" the emperor offered, removing a small tin from his vest and opening it. Willie and I took some of the candy.

"What do you say to Boney, Willie?" I said sternly.

"*Merci,*" the boy dutifully replied, pleasing the emperor with his French. Bonaparte mussed up his own hair and growled playfully at him. Willie doubled over in giggly hysterics.

My brothers were no longer afraid of "Boney." Judging by the black teeth they sported these days, the emperor had bribed them with licorice.

A deep, rich laugh boomed behind us.

"Betsy," the emperor said, "may I present Ensign Carstairs, my designated 'nanny *du jour.*'"

The man, who had apparently been standing in the corner watching us the whole time, winked at me. And I was astonished to realize that not only was this the handsome young soldier Jane was admiring from afar, but he was the same one who winked at me that day Huff and I had conspired near the banyan tree!

Carstairs bowed. "He means, Miss Balcombe," the fellow said, smiling mischievously, "that the admiral has sent me to keep an eye on this rascal for today."

Well, the man had gumption. Who else but I would think of calling the emperor a "rascal" to his face?

"Really, monsieur," the emperor replied, "you flatter me."

"Pleased to make your acquaintance, Miss Betsy," Carstairs said. He smelled of bay rum and horse sweat. To my astonishment, he kissed my hand, as if I were an Egyptian princess. No one had ever done that before. I had always thought such affectations silly, but for some reason, it didn't seem so ridiculous now.

I stared at Carstairs for so long, I was grateful when Willie started playing the piano again.

The emperor approached and held out his hand to me. "Dance, mademoiselle?"

Yes, this day was shaping up to be very surprising indeed.

I took the emperor's arm. He showed me some steps that were popular in Paris. His hand was even softer than I'd expected, as if he'd never lifted a hoe in his life.

"Ouch!" I said when he stepped on my toe.

"Don't be so clumsy, Betsy," he replied, as if it had been my fault.

Hoping to improve matters, I suggested I teach him some English dances—the ones Miss Hawthorne had taught the girls in London.

"Play us a waltz, Willie," I said. My brother complied.

"One-two-three—no!—*one*-two-three," I instructed my partner.

The emperor was an awkward student. The waltz refrains resulted in my getting my toes trounced again. So I tried the quadrilles. I am sorry to report that this went no better.

"In France," the emperor snapped, struggling to take control, "it is customary for the man to lead!"

"Well, Boney," I complained, "how will you ever learn if you don't let me teach you?"

"May I cut in?" Carstairs said, tapping the emperor on the shoulder.

"Why not?" the emperor said sourly. "She has the grace of a sow!" Still, it seemed to me that he stepped aside only grudgingly.

"You must not be so hard on him," Carstairs said to me, smiling. He danced with the grace of a gazelle. "Until he met you, his biggest challenge was the Russian army."

"Do not think I didn't hear that," the emperor called out.

"Why did you want to dance with me?" I asked the ensign, genuinely puzzled.

"Ah . . . ," he replied. "I am told you are wild, headstrong, irresponsible—a perfect terror!" He held me closer, and I felt a strange chill go up my spine. Not at all unpleasant, really. "Just my kind of girl," he said.

"Is that so? And who told you that about me?" I demanded, trying to sound indignant.

"We soldiers talk in the barracks at night, you know. There is not much else to do here. Most of the boys like Jane."

"Yes, I know," I said a bit disapprovingly.

"But her charms are too obvious for me," Carstairs said. "I prefer a challenge. And you, Miss Betsy, are a challenge!"

"Is that so?" I said again. "Really, you are an impertinent fellow."

"Yes, I know," Carstairs replied, spinning me around the room, faster and faster, till I burst out laughing. "Some say that is my best quality!" Carstairs was laughing too. And I couldn't help noticing the way his blue eyes sparkled like little lightning storms at sea when he looked at me.

The dance was over. I was amazed that I hadn't given a thought to the balloon for the past half hour. That was a good thing indeed, for the constant worry was rough on my nerves.

As I moved toward a chair, still breathing hard from my whirlwind dance with Carstairs, the emperor caught me by the arm and whispered in my ear. "He is too aristocratic for you, Betsy," he said.

I did not know what to make of his comment. Could it be possible that he, the former emperor of France, was jealous? Over Betsy Balcombe? For a brief instant I imagined the two men dueling over me. Or was it merely fatherly advice?

Just then Gourgaud entered the room at a march. He clicked his heels together and bowed. Really, was such a fuss necessary?

"Your Highness, Admiral Cockburn wishes to be announced."

"Send him in, Gourgaud," the emperor replied.

Admiral Cockburn acknowledged Carstairs and me with a nod. Poor Willie was ignored, as small children often are.

Cockburn told the emperor that the new governor, Sir Hudson Lowe, would be arriving shortly—sooner than expected.

"He will be relieving me of my duties here," the admiral added.

Bonaparte considered this in silence for a moment. I suppose he was wondering about his future.

"You shall be missed, Admiral," the emperor said at last. "As jailers go, you are *la crème de la crème*."

Cockburn smiled. "And as prisoners go, so are you," he replied.

The two men shook hands. It surprised me that some kind of mutual admiration had developed between them.

"They will be having a farewell party for me on Saturday," the admiral said to Bonaparte. "My staff will be surprising me with it, and I shall look appropriately surprised. You are invited to attend if you wish, General."

"The emperor," Bonaparte replied with emphasis, and a grin, "shall stay at home, *merci*. But he shall be present in spirit."

The admiral nodded in acknowledgment. As an afterthought, he looked at me and remarked, "You are invited too, Miss Balcombe. And your family."

"Thank you, sir," I said. "I shall give them the message."

Carstairs looked put out.

"And you are welcome also, Ensign," the admiral said.

Carstairs and I exchanged a smile at this bit of unexpected good fortune.

Cockburn turned to go. He was halfway out

the door when the emperor called to him. "Oh, Admiral?"

Cockburn spun around on his heel to face him, eyebrows raised in expectancy.

"What sort of man is this—this Hudson Lowe?"

The admiral paused. "A soldier, like yourself," he said at last, measuring his words carefully. "I believe he fought at Champaubert."

"Champaubert?" replied the emperor. "We probably fired guns at one another. For me that is always the beginning of a very happy relationship."

For my part, I wasn't so sure. But I consoled myself that as of tomorrow night, the emperor would be a free man.

Cockburn took his leave.

"It was . . . interesting conversing with you, Ensign Carstairs," I said.

"Likewise," Carstairs said, bowing.

"I suppose I shall be seeing you at the admiral's ball?" I ventured with unaccustomed timorousness.

"Plagues or typhoons couldn't keep me away, Betsy," he replied. I could not conceal my pleasure at this.

Bonaparte winced. I suppose Carstairs's dramatic language offended his literary sensibilities.

"Good-bye, Boney," I said, preparing to take

my leave. I needed to start collecting straw for the balloon's furnace.

"*Bonne chance*, mademoiselle," the emperor replied.

Good luck? How odd—how odd—that he used that phrase on this day of all days. He'd never said more than *adieu* to me before.

Chapter 12

P rovidence was with us and the weather promised clear sailing. The full moon cast a strong light over the beach. Huff and I had selected this remote spot on the island because few St. Helenians lived here and, shielded by a row of jagged mountains, there was little chance we'd be seen. Any soul wandering the beach, returning from a spree in Jamestown, would attribute the ghostly apparition of our flying contraption to too much rum—and surely vow to quit drinking forever.

The fire we'd made in the gondola was going furiously now, and the balloon slowly unfurled itself like a man stretching after a night's sleep.

"Hold back on the straw, Betsy," Huff told me. "Save the rest for the flight."

It was a grand sight. Huff, who was artistically inclined, had even seen fit to paint some decorations on the balloon's exterior—some lions' heads, as a subtle reference to its celebrated passenger. The name "Napoleon," Huff told me, means "lion of the forest."

Spectacular as it was, the balloon had been made so crudely—from so many different elements—that it looked more like a giant inflated quilt than any balloon the Montgolfiers would recognize. They had used linen for their balloon; Huff had insisted on silk for ours because he believed the tighter weave would hold the air better—for a far longer voyage.

At last we were ready. Huff and I filled several bags with beach sand for ballast.

"Ladies first," Huff said, holding the gondola steady so I could climb aboard. The basket danced a bit in the breeze as I put my foot in it. Our balloon strained at anchor, as if anxious to fly.

The old man joined me in the gondola. Then he cut the anchor rope, which had been tied to a stake, and fed straw to the furnace.

"Nothing is happening," I said.

"Is that so, my dear?" Huff said, teasing me. "Look down."

To my surprise, we were already a few feet off

the ground! I could see the smooth greenish carapace of a small sea turtle on the beach.

In no time at all we were far above the beach. Exhilaration! How can I ever find words to describe the feeling? It was as if I'd left my body on the ground and my soul was now free to sail among the stars with the immortals! Was this the complete freedom I had been seeking all my life? If not, it was as close to it as any human could ever expect to come.

The lights of Jamestown twinkled in the distance. I ducked instinctively as a booby suddenly flew by our balloon—close enough for me to have grabbed its webbed blue foot if I'd been so inclined. As we rose higher, I watched the wild pigs on the island turn from recognizable beasts into little black dots. Entire houses became nothing more than children's toy blocks. Farmers' green fields were empty chessboards. From up here, St. Helena could almost be called something no one had ever called it before: beautiful.

"Well? What do you think, Betsy?" Huff asked me, holding out his arms to encompass the whole exquisite panorama below us.

"I think—I think—" I searched for words. "I think I'd like to go with you! Please let me go with you, Huff!"

The old man laughed. He opened the cooling vent to let out a little air. We dropped slowly by a few feet, like a leaf gently drifting on the breeze.

"I wish I could, my dear, but the gondola is made to hold only two people. And a mutual friend of ours has a place reserved on it."

It may seem odd, but this was the first time that I really considered what life would be like for me without the emperor. I hadn't permitted myself to think of this before and I was struck with a terrible sadness. What a misery it would be to have only Jane for company! Until now I hadn't fully realized how much the emperor had brightened my days. And how unbearably dim life would seem without him.

"You look sad, my dear," Huff said, putting his hand on my shoulder.

I shook my head. "It's nothing," I replied, attempting a smile. I did not want to worry him.

The wind blew my hair in my eyes, and it was then that I realized the weather was changing. Huff didn't like the looks of things. Approaching the mountains, a cold blast of air came from them and dark clouds gathered over us, drifting in front of the moon. On St. Helena we have a saying: "If you don't like the weather, wait a few minutes; it'll change." The wind kicked up even more, and the

fire in the furnace was in danger of going out. Huff
rushed to add more straw to it.

"Quick, Betsy! Help me!"

We piled straw and wool scraps onto the fire as
quickly as we could. At first the fire flickered only
weakly, and we shielded the feeble flame from the
wind with our bodies. But, at last, much to our
relief, it gained strength and burned brightly again.

Just when we thought our worries were behind
us, I felt something flick my cheek.

Rain!

Before long the fire went out. We were sinking!

"Huff!" I shouted through the wind. "What'll
we do?"

Fortunately, he had had the presence of mind to
bring flints along with us. He struck one furiously
against a striker, trying to raise a spark.

"Find something that will burn!" he shouted
hoarsely.

I conducted a mad search for something dry to
light. The balloon was tumbling faster, drifting
over the sea. Wind and rain beating against my face,
I turned everything over, but there was little dry
straw in the gondola. Finally, I grabbed the hem of
my petticoat—thank heaven I'd chanced to wear one
that day—and ripped. This was no time for modesty.

Shielding the torn fabric from the rain, I held it next to the flint, waiting for Huff to strike a spark.

Then, miracle of miracles, the rain stopped, a spark caught, and the cloth fragment in my hand burst into flame.

"Ouch!" I quickly dropped the flaming cloth into the furnace. Slowly, fitfully, the dampish straw caught fire. Smoky, yes—but a fire nonetheless. The wind died down.

We gained altitude, far less quickly than I would have hoped, but we were rising.

Huff coughed from the smoke.

"Are you all right?" I asked him.

Before he could reply, we both heard a strange sound. It was a low, hissing noise, like the warning made by a snake.

"What is it, Huff?"

"Oh, dear." he said. "This is bad. Very bad, indeed."

"What's wrong?" I asked.

The hissing grew louder, and I realized, to my horror, that we had reversed course. We were no longer rising—we were sinking again!

By now I had figured out the source of our difficulty, and Huff confirmed my fears.

"A leak," he said, pointing to the upper part of the balloon. "The wind must have torn it!"

"Well, can't we fix it?" I said nervously.

Huff shook his head. "Too late," he replied. We were falling with increasing speed. The trees went by my vision in a blur.

"Lean toward shore!" Huff ordered. We were drifting toward the ocean again. I joined Huff at the port side of the gondola, and we threw all our weight in that direction. But the trade winds were blowing from the southeast, and despite our best efforts, we were headed out to sea.

I looked below us. The great blue ocean was coming up to meet us. We weren't far off shore, but at this rate we'd land in the drink.

"Throw off the ballast!" Huff shouted.

We threw the sandbags over the side. That slowed our descent, but wouldn't change the inevitable outcome.

"Betsy, if you know any prayers, I suggest you say them now," Huff said, kneeling down. I saw his lips moving as he mumbled piously.

I knelt beside him. One look over the side told me I'd better pray fast. But I knew no prayers. I bowed my head and clasped my hands as I'd seen my mother do in church.

"God! Oh, God, king of the universe, this is Betsy," I said. "Help!"

We hit the water like a cold slap.

All was dark. Not only did I find myself under water, but the balloon had collapsed over us. I couldn't breathe, and the cold water chewed through my bones like a hungry bear. Trapped!

The balloon wrestled with me—or so it seemed. I fought and struggled to free myself, but it was useless. And then, suddenly, a strange feeling came over me. It was more than one of resignation. It was peace. I stopped fighting.

I suppose I felt my life was not worth struggling to preserve. I had failed the emperor. And I was condemned to boredom on St. Helena, an empty future. No, this was not a life worth fighting for.

My limbs went limp. The sound of the ocean rushed in my ears. I floated free of the gondola. And then I saw a golden light. Was this heaven? Surely God's adjudicators had assigned me to the wrong place.

No, not heaven—but moonlight! My head bobbed above the surface of the ocean. I was alive! And despite my momentary despair, glad to be so. Perhaps I did have a purpose in life after all.

Perhaps God wanted me to live so I could try again to save the emperor!

"Huff! Huff!" I called out. I spun around in the water, looking every which way.

There was no sign of the old man. Though my teeth rattled with the cold, I swam out to the gondola again and again. I dived beneath the water's surface, struggling to keep my eyes open in the briny sting. My legs grew numb from the chill.

"Huff! Are you there?"

I heard a rushing sound and looked up. Dear God! A great, towering wave was poised over my head. In a flash I knew it would come crashing down on top of me. There was nothing for me to do. I covered my face and screamed.

The weight was like a thousand bricks. It dragged me toward the shore on my belly. Rough sand and broken seashells scraped my stomach raw. I was deposited facedown on the beach like a ragged bit of seaweed.

For a time I lay motionless, breathing hard. Then, despite the pain of my wounds, I pulled myself up on my elbows and knees. I coughed endlessly, and seawater poured out of my nose and mouth. My throat felt raw, afire. Exhausted, I flipped over onto my back like a struggling sea turtle.

"Huff!" I called out again.

But there was no trace of him. I scanned the surface of the ocean, hoping to see his head bobbing above it like a buoy, hoping against hope to hear that familiar voice call out, *I'm fine, my dear!*

But I saw nothing. The balloon and gondola had been washed far out to sea. *Perhaps,* I thought, *Huff has washed up alive on another beach where I can't see him. Yes, that's it!* He's waiting for me there, and when I find him, he will tap his foot and say, *Well, Betsy. Just like a woman to keep me waiting. . . .*

Right then I saw a familiar object bobbing on the waves.

"Huff! Thank God you're—"

But a second wave washed it up on the beach.

Huff's red fez.

That was all.

Chapter 13

"It was all my fault, Belle!" I said as we plodded back to the Briars. Every bounce of the saddle hurt my aching body. "If only I hadn't urged him to test the balloon before he was ready! If only I had listened to him about the weather. Huff would be alive now!"

Belle shook her head vigorously. I knew it was probably only a fly bothering her, but it was as if she were trying to say I shouldn't be so hard on myself.

"Belle! Whatever shall I do? Whatever shall I tell them?" I buried my face in her mane and wept.

It probably won't surprise you that Belle said nothing in reply.

"Of course, you are right," I said with a sigh. "I can say nothing at all. If I tell them how Huff died, they'd probably blame the emperor. No one would ever believe he didn't know of Huff's plans. They'd have Boney shot—and all the Balcombes as well!"

The lump of sugar I'd brought along with me for Belle had dissolved in the sea, so I could only pat her to show I appreciated her listening to my troubles.

"Wait! What if I merely told them that Huff and I went swimming and he got carried out to sea?" I said hopefully.

"Swimming at midnight? With the water as cold as it's been lately? You're right again, Belle. Half-truths would work no better. I will have to keep mum."

We were nearing home when I was overcome with emotion again.

"How can I keep this awful secret to myself? For the rest of my life? It will bury me under its weight."

We passed the Pavilion. Just then I got an idea.

"Boney! Why didn't I think of it before? I'll tell Boney!" I said, relieved. "After all, I owe it to Huff to tell the emperor that he gave his life for him."

I had never needed to speak to anyone so badly in my life. Rather than wake everyone up by knocking on the front door, I galloped up to the rear of the Pavilion, where Boney's room was located. I was so glad that I'd soon be able to talk to him that I gave no thought to the pain in my middle, the blood-stains on my dress, and my unkempt appearance.

I dismounted, climbed a tree, and peered through the upstairs window into Boney's room. The lamp was lit—he was still up. I raised my hand to knock on the glass.

But before I could rap on the window, someone entered the emperor's bedchamber. It was a woman in her nightdress! She paused for a moment in the doorway, then he smiled at her. She sat on the emperor's bed and put her arms around him. She kissed him! Then she turned to blow out the lamp, and I saw her face. Countess Montholon!

It was dark in the bedroom now. Still, I averted my eyes. I was sickened. Furious! After all I'd done for Boney, the one time—the *one* time—I needed him, he was carrying on with that trollop!

I walked Belle to the barn and gave her a rub-down. As I worked, my thoughts returned to the emperor. *Maybe I'm too harsh with him,* I mused. *He is entitled to some happiness, I suppose, is he not? Heaven knows he has little enough of it here.*

I resolved to forgive him. Though, of course, it would not be easy. No, not easy at all.

As I climbed through my bedroom window, I

wondered whether I should try again tomorrow to tell the emperor of poor Huff's sacrifice. And what of *my* sacrifice? Yes, what of mine? If he knew he was idling away the hours with his cheap mistress while I returned battered and bruised—and half drowned, to boot!—for his sake, how would he feel? Supremely repentant, no doubt! Would the countess have risked her pretty white neck for him? Don't make me laugh!

Ah, but I was losing my temper again. And I had resolved to forgive him, after all.

As I prepared for bed, I wondered how I'd tell the emperor of the balloon. And then, all at once, it became clear to me that I could *never* tell him. If I did, he would probably forbid me from attempting any such foolish escapades in the future. He would not want me risking my life for him again.

But risk my life I would do again—and again—if it would help set him free. Yes, it was clearly too late for me to build another balloon, even if I could do it without Huff's help. Bonaparte would be moved to Longwood soon, and the new governor would be arriving before the end of the week. But I vowed to try again to free the emperor, somehow, someday. Someday. . . .

I glanced over at Jane. Sleeping like a rock, as

usual. Whoever wrote of the "sleep of the just" never met my sister. With all the spiteful things she'd done in her life, by rights she should have been up every night, counting her sins.

But will she rat on me when she discovers Huff is dead? I wondered. I thought not. I doubted even Jane would be capable of such heartlessness.

I hid my wet dress in a bag so my mother wouldn't see the bloodstains. I'd wash it myself tomorrow.

I pulled up my nightdress and counted my war wounds. *Shall I get the Order of the Garter for this?* I winced and eased myself painfully into bed.

At breakfast the next morning no one spoke of Huff's disappearance. I imagined it would be some days—till Willie and Alexander's next tutoring session—before anyone would notice his absence.

"Betsy, is something wrong?" my mother asked me. She had seen me ease myself into a chair with the painful caution of an old lady with rheumatism.

"Nothing, Mother," I replied with my usual forthrightness. "Belle threw me yesterday. That's all."

"Nothing broken, I hope. Perhaps we shall have Dr. O'Meara take a look at you." She looked at my father for his approval. "William?"

But I didn't give my father a chance to reply. "No!" I said. Then, softening my tone, "I'm all right, Mother. Really."

She gave me a suspicious glance. "You haven't been riding astride again, have you?"

"Please pass the milk," I said to Willie, trying to avoid having to tell another lie. I endeavor to limit myself to one lie each day before lunch.

"I have some good news for you, Betsy," my father said. *I could use some of that.*

"Oh?" I said.

"Admiral Cockburn has made me purveyor to General Bonaparte and his suite." He grinned pridefully, as if he had just announced he was going to be coronated king of England.

"Purveyor?" I didn't know the meaning of the word. It was one of those stuffy ones.

My father explained. "I'll be in charge of securing supplies for the Frenchmen. Food, mostly. Cockburn wanted to make sure the general would be well looked after in his absence."

"Oh," I said, unimpressed.

I suppose Father thought I was feeling glum about Bonaparte's upcoming transfer to Longwood and that his news would cheer me up.

"Can you get him some more licorice?" Willie asked him.

Everybody laughed. Even my father.

Later that day, I volunteered to do all our washing, which pleasantly astonished my mother. But my real purpose was to scrub the bloodstains from my dress in secret.

That evening I dined with the emperor. It made me uneasy to have to sit across a table from Countess Montholon. But I simply ignored her whenever possible. She and the emperor did not steal amorous glances back and forth. If I hadn't seen things with my own eyes, I would have thought there was nothing between them. I suppose that's what they wanted Count Montholon to think too.

After dinner, we played whist. The emperor was the dealer, and I saw him slip an extra card to himself from under the deck.

"You cheated, Boney!" I declared.

Gourgaud ran to the emperor's side. "What?!" Gourgaud snapped at me. "How dare you speak to the emperor of France in such a manner! Why, you common little—"

"Now, now, Gourgaud," the emperor said. "She was only teasing. You are correct that I wasn't cheating. So there is no need to rush to defend me."

"Yes, you were," I said to Boney.

"That does it!" Gourgaud said, stamping his foot. "Sire, I will not stand here and let this miserable brat insult you!" Gourgaud looked like he was going to strike me. I was entirely prepared to hit him back if the situation called for it.

Marchand stepped between us.

"We shall play a less dangerous game than whist," the emperor said firmly. He collected the cards. And that, I thought, was that. I went home.

My parents seemed to be on a campaign to raise my spirits. And later that night my mother gave me a present. Little did she know all that had happened to me in the past twenty-four hours.

"Your first real ball gown," my mother said as I modeled it for her. "You look like a grown-up young lady," she said, misty-eyed. "And to think it seems just yesterday that I was rocking you in my arms!"

Normally, I wouldn't have stood still for such nonsense, but just this once I didn't mind having a pretty dress to wear. There was a certain young man I was looking forward to impressing at the admiral's ball. I changed back into my everyday clothes. But then I had a good notion. I decided to test my dress out—on Boney. He was old, but he'd have to do.

I walked over to the Pavilion wearing my regular frock and carrying the new one to show the emperor. I was too lazy to actually try it on again. Besides, I didn't want to risk dragging its train in the dirt outside.

Boney was reading aloud from Racine's *Iphigénie* when I walked in. I was more than a little grateful that I'd missed most of his soliloquy.

"What do you think?" I said, holding the ball gown up in front of me for his inspection.

"*Bien.* Very nice," he said. "For what occasion?"

"For the admiral's party Saturday." I smiled sheepishly and feared I might be blushing—a very un-Betsy-like state of affairs. "The ensign will be there, you know."

Bonaparte nodded.

And before I knew what I was about, he grabbed the dress right out of my hands.

"Call me a cheater, will you?" he said, laughing.

"Boney! Give it back right this minute," I ordered.

He shrugged and held it out to me. I reached for it. At the very last second he pulled it beyond my grasp and hid it behind his back.

"Not till you say you lied," he said, laughing at me.

Gourgaud and the others seemed to be enjoying all this immensely.

"I most certainly will not!" I said, indignant. "Hand it over."

"Mademoiselle looks very silly when she is angry, *n'est-ce pas*, Gourgaud?" he said. The rest of the group nodded to encourage Boney in his childish behavior.

Furious, I chased him around the furniture.

"*Toro! Toro!*" he said, waving the dress at me as if he were a Spanish matador and I the bull.

He was standing very close, taunting me. And then I had an inspiration.

I grabbed his sword right out of its scabbard.

"*Sacre bleu!*" said Gourgaud, horrified. Countess Montholon gasped.

I aimed the sword at the emperor's chest. I didn't intend to hurt him, of course. Just to make a . . . point.

"Frenchman, say your prayers!" I shouted. I think I'd once read that phrase in some book about pirates.

"Betsy, this is very serious," Bonaparte said. "That is the emperor's sword. Even Wellington did not take it from me. Return it at once!"

It was clear he was no longer amused. But then, neither was I.

"Sire, this is an outrage!" Gourgaud said.

"Give me my dress!" I demanded, unmovable. He studied me.

"Sword first," he replied, eyes flashing with penetrating sternness. "Surrender, mademoiselle."

All eyes were upon me. Some of the women looked frightened. The men seemed more nervous than scared. I began to realize that I had committed some sort of terrible transgression. I'd thought a sword was a sword. But not in the emperor's case, so it seemed. I'd have to set matters to rights.

I turned the gold hilt around to face him and passed the sword back to him.

"Sorry," I said. I held out my hands. "Now my dress."

The emperor tossed his sword back into the scabbard at his hip with a flourish. It made a steely *whoosh!*

Bonaparte looked very displeased with me.

"My dress," I said again. He did not respond. "Boney, this is not fair!" I said. "You promised."

But it was no use. The emperor laughed again like Puck, ran up to his bedchamber, and shut the door. I dashed after him and tried the knob. *Blast!* He'd locked me out!

For about five minutes I pounded on the door. I heard him chuckling softly to himself. Finally, I gave up and went home. Bonaparte was victorious. In one fell swoop the emperor had made up for his loss at Waterloo.

Chapter 14

I hardly spoke to anyone all the next day. And I'm rather ashamed to admit I spent the better part of two hours draped over my bed, brooding like a consumptive.

"But, Betsy," Jane argued as she did up her hair for the party, "why don't you wear your regular old party dress to the admiral's ball? You've worn it to every other occasion."

I wondered if she was trying to get in a subtle dig over my limited wardrobe.

"No!" I said. "This time is . . . different. I wouldn't be caught dead in that stupid little—"

"It's not so bad," Jane interrupted, mumbling from the hairpins in her mouth. "Mother thinks you look like a little china doll in that dress."

Looking like a little doll was the last thing I wanted, especially in front of Ensign Carstairs. I had no intention of going to the admiral's ball in a child's dress. I'd be damned if I'd go at all!

I lay on my bed, pounding my fists in frustration. If Boney could have seen me right then, he'd have felt even more triumphant than he had the previous night. Yes, I was a pathetic case. By dusk I pulled myself together and went downstairs—so no rumors would get back to the emperor that I was wasting away in misery over the theft of my dress.

I stepped outside for some air. It was a warm night, as most are on St. Helena the year round. It reminded me of all the evenings I'd spent talking to Huff under the banyan tree when I was younger. And it made me very sad to realize that there would be no more such nights.

Out of the corner of my eye, I saw Bonaparte sitting on the Pavilion veranda. It was dark now, and Willie and Alexander were sitting on the porch swing near the emperor. I went around the corner of the house to hide where they could not see me, and listened. Boney was terrifying the boys with ghost stories. From his native Corsica, I supposed. I heard only the tail end of one of the stories.

"And so," he concluded, "when the old owl screeches the night through . . ." Boney lowered his voice to a harsh whisper and then hooted like the owls I'd heard when visiting the English countryside. "When the mangy dog howls . . ." He imitated a wolf with a head cold. "And a pale yellow light appears over a man's house . . ." Here the emperor paused for dramatic effect and removed his straw hat, placed it over his heart, and bent his head as if in respectful prayer. ". . . he will be the next to die." Poor Willie and Alexander looked terrified. I'm sure this pleased the emperor very much.

I did not want to watch this ridiculous spectacle any longer, so I headed into Jamestown for a walk.

When I returned to the Briars, I found Jane downstairs, all dressed for the party. My parents had decided not to attend. My older sister had pleaded tearfully with them—Jane's crocodile tears never failed to work their magic on my parents—not to "chaperone" her, and they had given in to her wishes. I wondered if they knew just how badly Jane was in need of parental supervision.

"Are you sure you won't change your mind, Betsy?" my mother asked me. "Admiral Cockburn will be so disappointed not to see you there."

I found it difficult to believe that the admiral would recall that he'd invited me, much less notice my absence.

"Yes, Mother," I said. "I'm sure." My father patted me on the head as if I were Tom Pipes. Jane gathered up her wrap and purse and prepared to leave for the party.

Oh, the tragedy of it all! I was missing the party—and missing what would probably be my one and only chance to see Ensign Carstairs again. He was expecting me, I reasoned. *He'll think I'm snubbing him!* But, of course, I could never tell him the truth. What was I to say? That the emperor absconded with my dress and I had only an infant's monstrosity to wear in its place? He'd never take me seriously again!

"Well, I'm off!" Jane said, like an obnoxiously self-absorbed princess from some country I'd never like to visit.

"Have a good time, dear," my mother called after her. "Don't be home too late!"

Too late for what? I couldn't help thinking. My parents were already too late to preserve Jane's maidenhead.

Miserable beyond words, I shuffled my way upstairs. When I opened the door to my room, I was enraged to see that Jane had left one of her dresses on my bed again. How could I properly flop down in dejection with her stupid dress there?

I reached to pick it up. But, to my astonishment, it wasn't Jane's dress; it was mine. My new ball gown! Eagerly, I unfolded it. Yes, it was good as new. How had it gotten here?

Just then I heard something hit the floor. A heavy object had fallen out of the folds of the dress. I bent to pick it up. *Hello, what's this?* A necklace! With diamonds and sapphires!

There was a note pinned to the peplum of my dress.

The necklace was Joséphine's.
It is yours for the evening.
—Boney

I was stunned. The emperor's generosity almost made up for his bad behavior. Almost.

With trembling hands, I held the necklace up to my neck and examined myself in the looking glass. Imagine! Of all the girls in the world, he had chosen me to wear the jewels of the empress of France!

I never dressed so fast as I did that night. In a flash I ran downstairs in my bare feet.

"Mother! Please do my hair for me? I'm going to the party after all."

"Well," my father replied for her, "I knew you'd come to your senses."

Mother obliged me by putting my hair up in a bun.

"Hold still, Betsy!" she said as she put in the pins. "You'll get stuck!"

I jiggled nervously, like an organ-grinder's monkey. I was worried about the time. If I didn't get to the party soon, perhaps Carstairs would give up and go home.

As Mother worked on my hair, I had time to wonder again: How had my dress managed to end up on my bed? Who brought it there? The emperor was not permitted to come and go as he pleased.

"Mother, did anyone stop by the house this evening?"

"No," she said. "Why?" I looked at my father questioningly, and he shook his head. Neither had seen anyone come in—and Jane would have mentioned it if we'd had any visitors.

"No reason," I answered. I did not want to get anyone in trouble. But the matter of how Bonaparte had managed to smuggle my dress to me would forever remain a mystery. To my eternal frustration, he always refused to tell me.

My parents were impressed by the appearance I made in my new dress. Of course, I hid the necklace in the palm of my hand so they wouldn't question me about it. I bade them a hurried good-bye and went to the party.

Plantation House, dark for so many years, was lit up like a big, beautiful birthday cake. When I entered the crowded ballroom, I was swept away by beauty and music and light, and over by the piano—oh, joy of joys!—Carstairs was there, as I had hoped. He'd waited for me! Carstairs held out his arm—bowing slightly in his crisp, handsome dress uniform—and we danced and danced till late into the night. He ignored poor Jane and all the rest—even girls prettier than I, which I confess was most of them. I felt like Joséphine herself!

Sometime before the first waltz and the last quadrille, Carstairs took me outside, led me behind a column on the porch, and . . .

Well, some things are just too sacred to expose to the prying eyes of one's readers. Suffice it to say that my first brush with romance led me to conclude that no girl had ever been kissed with such total devotion, such complete capitulation, such passionate resolution.

"May I call on you sometime?" Carstairs asked as we parted.

I didn't reply. I was drifting, flying, careening, too overwhelmed to think clearly. I stared at him, feeling besieged by my own capabilities.

"If you don't say yes, I shall have to kiss you again," Carstairs joked.

"Oh," I said. "Please do!"

"Call on you?"

"No—kiss me!" I said, pulling him near to me.

"Not now, little one," he said, taking a step backward. I pouted, a bit put out that he had called me "little." "We shall save that for the next time we meet. I would not want to forget myself with you."

We parted, our hands hanging on until the last. First wrists, then palms, then knuckles, until our fingertips only touched like God giving Adam the spark of divine life in the painting by Michelangelo.

I floated back to the Briars, living all the while in a glorious, golden land within myself—a place of peace and freedom and autonomy.

As I drifted home, I took one last glance back at the spot that for me would forever have historical significance. The party lanterns hanging outside Plantation House waltzed prettily in the breeze.

Faded music and laughter from the house reached my ears like a distant dream.

And then, much closer, I heard the sound of someone clearing his throat. I looked up.

It was the emperor, sitting on the Pavilion veranda. He seemed to be scowling at me.

I curtsied to him. Odd, I thought, that he'd be outside so late.

"Good evening, monsieur."

I suspect he was a bit taken aback by my unusually formal behavior toward him, but he did not say so.

"Your *maman*, she wanted you home early," Bonaparte scolded me lightly, and I had the strangest feeling that he had been watching me all evening.

"It is early!" I replied, spinning in dizzy pirouettes. "I doubt it is more than an hour into the day!"

He clucked at me with the hint of a smile. I smiled back.

The emperor did not know quite what to make of me.

"Did you drink any port?" he asked me, uneasy.

"They don't serve port at parties!" I flopped down in a chair next to him.

"Well, not to the children, perhaps," he replied.

To the children! Offended, I got up to leave, but his voice stopped me.

"Did you—," the emperor began, hesitant. I turned back to face him. "Did you dance with anyone?"

I determined not to make his task easy for him. After all, what business was this of his? Standing up, I danced in dreamy circles about the lawn.

"Ah, oui," the emperor said, sadly humorous. "I see."

I could not know what he was thinking just then. But now that, as I write these words, I am no longer young, I can guess that he was feeling rather old.

The emperor yawned. Dizzy from my spinning, I nearly landed in a heap on the grass. I glanced toward Plantation House, with its brilliant rocking lanterns.

"Look at them!" I said, pointing. "Like someone caught the fireflies and put them in jars! Like someone caught stars!"

"The stars are in jars!" Bonaparte sang, imitating me. "The stars are in jars!"

"Don't make fun of me," I said.

The emperor nodded.

"And don't sing," I added.

He shrugged. I ignored him and stood up. I did my pirouettes. He watched me dance.

"Betsy," he said with intensity, "you look very . . ." I glanced up at him expectantly. He seemed to recover his reserve. ". . . appropriate tonight."

I can't say I wasn't disappointed. He had led me to expect some sort of daring compliment. My face showed my displeasure.

Still, I sat down next to him again. We were silent, awkward with each other as never before.

"Licorice?" he said, offering me some from his tin.

I shook my head. I looked toward Jamestown, its lights twinkling in the distance. The clouds above it drifted apart, revealing the same glorious golden moon I'd seen the night Huff had died. But even the sad and painful memories revived by that sight could not ruin the glory of this moment. Oh, how I hoped Huff, wherever he was, would forgive me for feeling so happy!

"There's never been a night—not ever! So bright!" I exulted.

"Garlands of light," Bonaparte said. He appeared to be lost in a dream of his own. "Diadems of light. The trees, the city, ablaze with light."

"Yes!" I said, surprised that he, too, understood the specialness of this night.

"The Great Silver Star over Place de la Concorde," he continued. "Twenty-two steps, up—up—to the throne of the Golden Bees."

Puzzled, I turned to face him. It was clear he was not speaking of this night, but of another, long ago. I listened intently as he wove his magic spell.

"Fireworks!" he said, waving his hands in the air. "First blue, then white, then red—exploding across the night! Ka-boom! Ka-boom! Ka-boom-boom! One thousand singers, one thousand dancers—and all of France crying, *'Vive l'Empereur! Vive l'Empereur!'*"

The emperor floated back down to earth from the heights to which the crowd had raised him. Slowly, he became aware of my presence once more.

I looked at him, thinking, wondering.

"That—," he explained, "that was the brightest night, my young one. The coronation—Notre Dame, Pope Pius VII, the crown of Charlemagne!" Here he spoke softly, enmeshed in more tender memories. "And Joséphine—sweet and matchless Joséphine . . ." He leaned way back in his chair and sighed. "That night, we danced; I held her in my arms. The crowd stepped back, gave us room. The empress!"

As he spoke, I saw her in my mind's eye—and saw myself as she. I, the empress! I, Joséphine. Dancing in the arms of Napoleon the Great, who, for that one special night, had a grace on the dance floor that he had never exhibited before—or since. After all, it was only a dream. Why spoil it with his clumsiness?

"I remember the feel—the silk of her dress against my arm," Bonaparte continued, brushing his hand lightly across his wrist. "The feel of Joséphine! Her perfume . . ." He sniffed the air and sighed with ecstasy. "Jasmine as she moved. Sandalwood when she stood still. The cape trimmed with ermine—soft; not as soft as that sweet skin. The crown, her diamonds, fires like her eyes. No, not as bright! Not as bright . . ."

He fell silent, as if the memory had crossed over some invisible line and was now bringing him more pain than joy. I did not know how to reach him in that place.

"My head hurts," I said. It was the truth, and as something to say, it seemed harmless enough.

"I am not surprised," the emperor replied. "After all that dancing."

"Thank you for the necklace," I said, undoing

the clasp and handing it back to him. "It is very beautiful."

He nodded. I stood up and walked toward the Briars.

"Whist tomorrow?" I called out to him from some feet away.

He nodded again.

"No cheating!" I said. The emperor attempted to appear stern, but I suspect he was actually smiling.

I ran toward the house, all girlish arms and legs.

"Good night, Boney!" I called as I rounded the bend.

"*Bonne nuit*, mademoiselle!" he called out to me.

I don't know what made me do it, but I stopped in my tracks. An impulse to turn around had taken hold of me. And, to my astonishment, when I did, I saw the emperor standing up on the veranda, bowing toward me as he would to . . . well, to an empress!

I smiled beatifically at him and curtsied.

And now I walked—slow and ladylike—toward home.

Chapter 15

The first indication I had of Governor Lowe's arrival on St. Helena came two days after the admiral's ball. I found myself imprisoned in the wine cellar. And it gave me a taste of just what sort of man the emperor's new jailer promised to be.

No, it wasn't Governor Lowe himself who tossed me in that dungeon. It was, rather uncharacteristically, my father. But it soon became clear that it was Lowe who was really behind my punishment.

It seems that someone—and the "someone" I suspected was Gourgaud—had been very upset by my daring to turn the emperor's sword against him some nights earlier. And Lowe had hardly had time to unpack his first trunk before he received a written complaint about the unruliness of one Betsy

Balcombe. While I was in Jamestown the previous day, the new governor had paid a call on my parents. Lowe informed them that he would be tightening security around the emperor and his suite and that his plans did not include young English girls waving swords around his prisoners. He recommended to my father that he administer some rather harsh punishment to his child so that she would be taught a lesson. It was Willie, my favorite "spy," who later told me of these events.

I suppose my father did not want to start out on the wrong foot with the new governor, so, reluctantly, he agreed to punish me. And I was sentenced to spend a day in purgatory, with only rats and my father's wine bottles for company.

It seemed another Betsy Balcombe entirely who, just forty-eight hours before, had been dancing in a beautiful ball gown, in the arms of a handsome soldier. How I wished Carstairs would come and rescue me! But there was little chance anyone but Lowe and my family knew of my current plight. And I suspected that Gourgaud had intentionally withheld the news from the emperor, so my friend could not comfort me.

It was only by chance—so I learned later—that the emperor discovered my situation. As he was walking by the Briars—escorted by Poppleton, of course—he heard a loud crash. It sounded like glass breaking, and it seemed to be coming from the cellar. Bonaparte asked the captain to dismount and take a look through the window.

"It's the Balcombe girl," Poppleton reported to his charge. He couldn't fail to notice that I was surrounded by broken wine bottles.

"Which one?" Boney said. I suppose if it were Jane, he wouldn't have bothered to investigate any further.

"The less attractive one," Poppleton replied.

If I hadn't been "feeling no pain," as my father's navy friends liked to say, I'd have been enraged by the captain's tactlessness. But to be perfectly frank, I had consumed nearly a whole bottle of my father's best Riesling and was in a grand and forgiving frame of mind.

Poppleton peered through the window bars at me.

I hiccuped and winked at him. "Helloooo, sailor!" I said.

Poppleton winced and turned his head, as if my breath offended him. "I think you had better talk to her, sir," Poppleton told the emperor.

Boney asked me how on earth I had come to be

in the cellar. I told him the whole story—how he could understand my slurred speech, I'll never know—and by the end my excessive joviality had turned into a crying jag.

He reached for my hand through the bars. "There, now, mademoiselle," he said, comforting me. "Now we are both prisoners, and you cry. I don't cry."

"You have," I replied.

"Yes," Boney said. "But the prison remains a prison. So it is better to be cheerful."

"I don't like Ssssir Ludson Showe," I complained.

The emperor laughed at my tipsy speech.

"Don't cry," he said. He pushed his handkerchief through my prison bars. I took it from him, dabbed my eyes, and passed it back. "Remember, Betsy, I understand all you say and do. Yes, more than your parents, perhaps. When you are liberated, come to me and we shall have my chef make some bonbons and we shall laugh again!"

I was grateful to him for his kindness. But after that I fell asleep rather suddenly before I could tell him so.

Some hours must have gone by because when I awoke again, it was dark and the emperor was gone.

Thank goodness I was sober by the time my father released me from "jail."

Before his arrival I hid the empty bottle behind some full ones and swept the broken glass to the side.

The next day, I awoke with a headache like a thousand bees had taken up residence in my brain. My mouth felt dry and cottony, as if it had been plugged with a very tiny mattress, and even the slightest bit of light hitting my eyes was as blinding as a thousand suns. The emperor was heartless enough to be amused by my experience of the aftereffects of drunkenness.

He was playing *colin-maillard*—what we English call "blindman's bluff"—with Willie and Alexander at the Pavilion (I felt too much under the weather to do more than watch) when Bertrand arrived with an announcement. It was a letter from Governor Lowe, the grand marshal explained, and required His Majesty's immediate attention. Willie untied the emperor's blindfold so he could open and read the letter. As he read it to himself, I watched Boney's expression alter from one of merriment to outrage.

"Surely the man is not serious!" the emperor said. "Listen to this, Bertrand." He read the note aloud: "'In addition to the regulations enacted by Rear Admiral Sir George Cockburn, K.C.B., it is further explicitly declared that no person is to receive or be the bearer of any letters or communications from General Bonaparte and the officers of his suite, or to deliver any to them. Any persons transgressing this order will be immediately arrested and otherwise dealt with accordingly by command of His Excellency Lieutenant General Sir Hudson Lowe, K.C.B., governor and commander in chief . . .' et cetera, et cetera." Bonaparte crumpled the letter and tossed it into the fireplace.

Bertrand addressed all of us. "Can you imagine how this pompous ass announces a trip to the latrine?" he said. "'I, Sir Hudson Lowe, lord and master of the universe, et cetera, et cetera, do hereby announce that I am going to relieve my glorious self!'"

Everyone laughed, but I suspected that under that laughter was more than a little concern about how life would change for the exiles now that Lowe was at the helm.

The next morning, I was writing a letter to Madeline, my only friend from school (who was still residing in London), when I was briefly interrupted by a knock on my door.

"Have you seen Huff?" my mother asked me. It seemed he was two hours late for his tutoring session with the boys, she explained, and it wasn't like the old man to be so unpunctual.

I told her the truth: that I had no idea where he was. After all, how could I know where the old man, may he rest in peace, was at that moment?

Some time later, my mother grew so concerned that she had my father look for Huff. When the landlady at Huff's lodgings in Jamestown avowed that she hadn't seen the old man in days, my father organized a search party. The searchers combed the island. At last, when no trace of Huff could be found, my parents concluded that he had been killed by one of the wild boars that roamed St. Helena. Huff had always had a tendency to wander off at odd hours and in odd places, and the explanation seemed to them as plausible as any.

We held a lovely service for him and buried him in absentia under a banyan tree. Willie and Alexander were very sad at Huff's loss. My father said Dr. O'Meara had volunteered to serve as the boys' tutor until a proper replacement could be brought in from London.

If I sound rather cold and detached as I relate these events, it is only because I had been mourning for Huff for some days by the time they occurred and had no more tears left to weep.

On the afternoon of Huff's funeral Governor Lowe and one of his aides, a Mr. Reade, showed up unannounced at the Pavilion. Lowe had never met the emperor face-to-face before. The governor rapped on the door. Gourgaud opened it. I was visiting with the emperor in the other room.

"Hudson Lowe is here, Sire," Gourgaud told him. "He says 'Mr. Bonaparte' will stop whatever he is doing immediately and receive him."

"Oh, he does, does he?" the emperor said, more than a little annoyed. "Tell him that the emperor will receive him when Monsieur Lowe learns some proper respect." Gourgaud returned to the front door.

"The emperor is indisposed," we heard Gourgaud transmit to the governor and his aide. In a moment Gourgaud returned to us with another message.

"The governor says, indisposed or not, you will see him or pay the consequences."

That did it. I hadn't seen the emperor so angry since the day after he arrived on St. Helena. His left thigh twitched—from an old war wound, he once told me—his eyes turned cold, and he drummed his fingers on the table. But he made no reply.

"What—what shall I tell him, Your Majesty?" Gourgaud said uneasily. I think Boney's anger always made the man a bit nervous.

"*Rien*," the emperor said with finality. "Such impertinence is not worthy of a reply."

Gourgaud seemed satisfied by this. The governor was going to be completely and utterly ignored.

Boney suggested a round of reversis. But it was not easy for me to concentrate on a game amid the racket coming from the front of the Pavilion. Every few seconds Reade would pound furiously on the door, and the whole house would shake as if we were experiencing an earthquake. And every now and then, we'd hear the governor yell, "I demand— I order you—to open up, Bonaparte! In the name of the Crown!"

I left the card game so I could peek through the curtains in the next room. Reade and the governor were standing on the veranda, steam almost visibly coming out of their ears. And the governor's appearance? I must say, Lowe couldn't have looked more like I'd expected him to if he'd been an actor cast to play the part. He was thin, with a long, scraggly neck like a rooster on half rations. His hair was faded yellow—almost dirty, as if he were in want of a bath. Lowe's cheeks were sunken, angular—I suppose God hadn't seen fit to give him more than the minimum allotment of human flesh—and covered with freckles and ugly brown blotches. It seemed as if he had some sort of skin disease that would excite more revulsion than pity. He had the kind of face that could only have been earned from a just deity, by a lifetime of misdeeds.

"The *docteurs* must soak him in sulfur and mercury," the emperor remarked disdainfully. "And *regarde*—those hyena's eyes of his!" I hadn't noticed Boney join me in spying on Lowe through the curtains. We watched the governor confer with Reade, and although we couldn't hear what Lowe said, I could tell a great deal about him by his stiff, affected way of moving, his nervous twisting, and false smile. Yes, Sir Hudson Lowe was a born jailer.

We heard the sound of rain beginning to spatter on the rooftop. In a moment it turned into a deluge. And Lowe and Reade stood outside in the downpour, shouting, pounding in vain on the front door, appearing more every moment like two very large and uncommonly ugly drowned rats.

Boney and I giggled over this spectacle, but I couldn't help wondering if he had acted in his own best interests by enraging this powerful personage.

After all, it was Lowe who now held the keys to his prison.

After another ten minutes the house no longer shook with the sounds of Lowe's pounding fists. He and Reade had gone home.

When the rain stopped a couple of hours later, Boney suggested we go for a ride. "Come," he said. "I need some fresh air."

While Boney got Hope from the barn, I went for Belle.

"I was sorry to hear about Monsieur Huff," the emperor told me as we saddled up upon my return. I started at hearing the old man's name. Apparently, one of Boney's staff had told him the news during my brief absence. "My condolences to you and yours, mademoiselle."

"Merci," I said. "We are all very sad."

"Old as he was," the emperor continued, "he had only just begun. Had Huff lived, he would have done great things."

I was struck by the irony of Boney's remarks. Was he referring to Huff's work on the Rosetta stone? Or perhaps to . . . something else? But I said nothing and merely nodded in agreement with him.

We had not ridden more than a hundred feet

from the Pavilion veranda when Poppleton galloped up seemingly out of nowhere and blocked our path. It was nearly impossible to avoid a collision. I screamed. The emperor and I pulled up on the reins with all our might—just in time. Hope reared up, whinnied in terror, and crashed to earth again— still on his feet, thank heaven. The impact of his hooves kicked up a blinding spray of mud.

"*Cochon!* You fool!" Bonaparte said to Poppleton, cursing and sputtering. "Watch where you're going!"

"Sorry, sir," the nervous young man replied.

"Poppleton! I have a young girl with me," the emperor said. "Have you gone mad? You could have killed us all!"

"As I said, sir, I ask your forgiveness."

"Hmmpphht!" Boney said, motioning for Poppleton to get out of the way.

Poppleton didn't move.

"Well? *Vite!*" the emperor said. "What are you waiting for? Make way!"

"I—I'm sorry, sir," Poppleton said again. "I can't. Governor's orders."

"What!?" the emperor demanded. "What are you talking about?"

"Governor Lowe has ordered me to stop you if

you ride beyond this line." He pointed to a miniature Union Jack stuck on a pole in the ground.

"Impossible!" Boney said, incredulous. "You mean to say the emperor of France is not at liberty to go riding on his own horse in broad daylight? I have ridden *tous les jours de ma vie*—every day—for forty years!"

"I'm afraid so, sir," Poppleton replied sheepishly. "Not past this point. Governor's orders."

The emperor gnashed his teeth. "Why, that— that—!"

"Uh, we'll be turning back now, Captain," I said, breaking in. I tugged at Boney's sleeve. He scowled at me but said no more. "We were—we were going home now anyway."

Chapter 16

My father once told me, "Betsy, change is like a storm at sea. If you do your duty, strap yourself to the mast and hold your ground, you'll weather the storm all right. But cower in fear belowdecks, the ship will be torn asunder—and you'll find yourself in the cold confines of the briny deep."

This, I suppose, was a long way of saying that if you don't make way for change, it'll sink you. And in the weeks after Governor Lowe's arrival, I certainly did come to feel that I was on a sinking ship. For the emperor and me, both, the new governor—with all his petty regulations and degrading restrictions— had brought storms to our sea of tranquility. Boney and I grew closer, clear in the unspoken knowledge that time was short and we would soon be separated.

Longwood would soon be ready to accept its new prisoner.

The only bright spot for me in this tempestuous seascape was the hope that Ensign Carstairs would sail into my life again. Each day I arose with the expectation that this—this!—would be the day of our long-awaited reunion. He sent me notes, explaining that try as he might, he could not get leave to come see me. I wrote back, with all the romantic outpourings of my youthful soul. But see him, I could not. The governor had restricted civilian access to the military encampments. So, as 1815 plodded slowly into 1816, and my wallowing winter dragged its way into soggy spring, I waited. And waited.

It was on a Wednesday morning in the spring of 1816 when an event occurred that I shall always remember with horror. The day began innocently enough. My family and I were eating breakfast in the dining room, and the boys were fighting over the last scone. Suddenly, we heard the door burst open like cannon fire.

My father, and all of us, immediately sprang from our seats.

Governor Lowe was standing in the doorway holding a slave roughly by the arm. The poor man's other arm was bent painfully at the elbow, pinned behind his back. Tears rolled down his smooth cheeks. The man was in leg irons. I gasped in horror when I saw who the prisoner was.

"Toby!" I was stricken. My eyes sent him a message that his pain was my pain, his suffering, mine. I ran to my father and clasped his waist, imploring. "Father, Father, please do something!"

"Shhh, Betsy!" my father said. But he was as angry as I, that was clear. He strode toward Lowe. "Governor, what is the meaning of this? Release him!"

"As you wish," Lowe replied. He sent Toby spinning across the floor, leg irons clattering noisily against the wooden boards. Toby landed in a heap at my father's feet, and I ran to his side.

"Toby, what have they done to you?" I said, trying to comfort him. I shook with fear. "What have they done!" His arms bore the cruel marks of Lowe's tentacles.

"Is all right, missy," Toby whispered to me. "Everything soon be all right now." With all the pain he was in, Toby was comforting me!

"Does this man belong to you?" Governor Lowe demanded of my father.

Father looked at the governor with disgust. "He

belongs to himself," my father snapped. "He works for me."

"Well, then, I see I have come to the right place," Lowe said with oily smoothness. He paused and methodically removed his gloves, as if he were planning to stay for a nice little visit. The governor turned toward my mother and smiled charmlessly. "Don't bother to put tea on for me, Mrs. Balcombe. What I have to say to your husband will only take a moment."

Of course, my mother had had no intention of doing any such thing.

Tom Pipes approached Lowe's pants leg. He sniffed at him, bared his fangs, and growled, low and threatening—as if he were facing down a rat in the barn.

"Nice doggie," Lowe said, patting our Tom on the head. He fed him a tidbit from his pocket. Tom—traitor that he was—stopped growling. My stomach roiled in revulsion. I reminded myself to give Tom a bath after this encounter—as I always did after his scuffles with skunks.

"I'm quite the animal lover, you know," Lowe said, as if any of us gave a damn. "I understand you have horse races here, is that not so? I'll look forward to running my Nelson in one of them." He stroked Tom, cooing kindly to him, as if this were a pleasant social call on his good friends, the Balcombes.

"State your business!" my father said. I was amazed by his restraint. But Lowe had contacts with my father's employer, the East India Company, and he knew he must watch his step.

Lowe abruptly removed an envelope from his military jacket. "This letter, addressed to Marie-Louise in Austria, was found hidden on your man there," the governor said, pointing to Toby. "He was caught trying to sneak aboard the *Northumberland* as it was getting ready to sail out of Jamestown last night."

Marie-Louise? That was Boney's wife! My father did not look as surprised as I would have expected him to.

"The communication is signed by the Frenchman," Lowe continued. He opened the letter, turned it rapidly to the last page, and handed it to my father. "Napoleon," he said, pointing to the signature. "That is in direct violation of my orders! Did your daughter transport this letter to that slave on behalf of the prisoner? Answer me!" the governor demanded.

"She most certainly did not," my father replied.

Well, it was nice to see him defending me. And then he said the most astonishing thing. "I did."

My mother gasped. And Lowe couldn't have looked more surprised if you'd told him he was first in line to succeed to the throne.

William Balcombe? Smuggling letters for the emperor? I wouldn't have thought him capable of such intrigue. But I must have gotten my devious mind from somewhere.

"Balcombe," Lowe said at last, pacing the floor and twitching nervously, "I suppose you know that by delivering this letter for the prisoner, you are in direct violation of my orders—which is to say, in direct violation of His Majesty, King George III, of whom I am the appointed representative on this island?"

"I do," my father replied forthrightly. I had to give him credit for courage.

My mother took a deep breath, preparing herself for the worst. Suddenly, it was all too much for her, and she swayed from side to side like a drunken sailor. Then, hand to her forehead, she moaned and—

"Mother!" Willie shouted, frightened. I ran toward her, but my father got there first. He caught her just before she hit the floor. Father carried her to the couch.

Willie fanned her with an arithmetic book he was carrying. My father sent Alexander for some water.

At last my mother's eyes fluttered and opened.

"Are you all right, my dear?" my father said, patting her hand. Mother smiled wanly.

"What has happened?" she said, still woozy.

"Everything's all right now. I'm here," he replied.

Father kissed her forehead. She squeezed his hand. I had rarely seen such a display of affection between them.

Father turned to Hudson Lowe. "Have you anything further to say, Governor?" he said, glaring.

Even Lowe seemed a bit cowed by my mother's accident. "Just this," he replied, struggling to recover his dignity. "I'll let you off this time, Balcombe, in deference to your wife." I breathed a sigh of relief. But Lowe wasn't finished. "But I warn you, sir. If you, or any member of your family"—he looked directly at me—"help the Frenchman again in any manner, there will be hell to pay!"

Lowe grabbed the emperor's letter rudely from my father's hands, tore it into pieces, and dropped them on the floor. With that, he spun on his heel and was gone, slamming the door in his wake.

No one in my family discussed the incident after that. My mother quickly recovered and spent the rest of the morning nursing Toby back to health. I didn't dare ask my father anything about how Boney had come to entrust him with his letter. Or why Father had chosen Toby, his most valued slave, to deliver it to Austria. The emperor had lost his only chance to reach his wife and son with a letter. But Toby had lost far more: his chance to be a free man.

The rest of the day passed without incident. But that night . . .

"Betsy," Jane said as she sat in front of the looking glass, giving her tresses the requisite hundred strokes with the hairbrush. "I shall offer you some sisterly advice."

With Jane, I had come to understand that "sisterly advice" was synonymous with spitefulness.

"Yes, Jane?" I said. "Please do it quickly." I yawned. "I want to go to sleep."

"I think you are seeing entirely too much of General Bonaparte."

"What business is that of yours?" I snapped.

"No need to get all huffy about it," Jane said. "I'm just thinking of your welfare. The boys at the barracks are talking about you, you know. And Governor Lowe doesn't like it either."

"Well?" I said, shrugging. "What are they saying?"

Jane put her brush down and blew out the lamp. She got into bed. "Perhaps when you are older," she said, her voice dripping with condescension, "I shall explain it to you."

"I'm not stupid, Jane," I said. "I know just what you're implying. But I don't believe you."

"Oh, no?" she replied. "Why do you think Ensign Carstairs is so interested in you?"

I flinched. *Jane knows about me and Carstairs! Well,* I reasoned, *she did see us dancing together at the party, after all.*

"So that's what this is all about!" I said, triumphant. "You're jealous of me and Carstairs!"

"Don't be silly, Betsy," Jane said, not too convincingly. "That has nothing to do with it. I'm just worried about you, is all. The boys in the barracks think that if that canny old Frenchman sees something in you—heaven knows I don't understand what it could be—you must be quite a hussy."

It takes one to know one.

"Oh, do shut up, Jane," I said. Her comments were not worthy of a more polite response. Only a fool would think there was anything improper between me and the emperor!

"Suit yourself," Jane replied.

I rolled over and went to sleep.

The next morning, just to infuriate Jane, I suppose, I made sure to visit the emperor. I told Boney about the terrible events involving his waylaid letter to Marie-Louise. He was outraged by Lowe's rampage against Toby and my family, and vowed to do something about it.

Just then Bertrand entered the room. "Some newspapers for you, Sire," he said, placing a roll of them on the table. "From Paris."

An old army friend had sent them to Boney and, I suppose, since the newspapers did not qualify as "correspondence," they were not intercepted by Lowe. The gazettes were months old—already beginning to yellow around the edges—but the emperor sat down and unrolled one excitedly, gingerly, eagerly, as if it were an original copy of a precious historical document like the Magna Carta.

He put on his spectacles and read the papers to me aloud. One article was about the price of butter in Paris. Another was about the declining health of King George III.

"Ah!" he said, perusing the back pages of one paper. "Here is an article about me. And it mentions you, too, Betsy."

"Really?" I said, quite thrilled. "Read that one!"

He translated for me: "'The former Emperor Napoleon, now held prisoner on the island of St. Helena located some twelve hundred miles off the coast of southwest Africa . . .' blah, blah, blah," he began, skipping ahead. "Ah! Here we go. 'He is seen frequently in the company of a spirited English nymph, Betsie Balcombe.' They spelled your name wrong; ah, well," he said, shrugging. "That's the press for you."

"Go on!" I said, thrilled that my name was being read all over Paris. "Read the rest."

He continued. "'In all the cafés it is possible to hear people wondering how France's Old Soldier, who by all accounts has grown quite round about the middle'—well, I like that!—'could have convinced this dainty piece to become his—'"

Abruptly, the emperor stopped reading. He seemed to be very uncomfortable. "*C'est tout*. That's all," he said. "I suppose the rest is missing."

"I don't believe you," I said, snatching the article from him and reading it silently to myself.

I knew enough French to know they were calling me his mistress. I was mortified. This very moment, I, Betsy Balcombe, was being sniggered about like a common courtesan—my name bandied about all over Paris!

Hot tears of anger and shame burned on my cheeks. I had to know the truth.

"Do you think of me?" I asked him. "That way, I mean?"

The emperor, troubled, looked down at his hands and sighed.

"Do you?" I demanded.

"Betsy, if I thought you were still a little girl, I would say—I could say no. No, I never think of you; never. But now it is different, you are older, more a woman—and know better than to believe what little girls believe."

He glanced up at me. I shook my head slowly, not wanting it to be true. I covered my ears. I wouldn't listen to any more of this. I was shocked, hurt. More than anything else, I felt he'd betrayed me.

Gently, Boney removed my hands from my ears. "You are different now," he continued. "Others, too, will change. They, too, have that right! What we are together will stay just the same as always—yes, the same, nothing more. But people will talk, as maybe they should. And you must care what they say, Betsy. You must care."

"No!" I said, overwhelmed by pain and confusion. "I don't care! If I meant anything to you—you wouldn't care either!"

I ran, crying, from the room and out the front door of the Pavilion.

"Betsy! Betsy!" the emperor called after me, helpless, helpless as he had never been when at the head of his army. But he knew he would be stopped by the guards if he tried to follow me.

Besides, at heart Boney probably knew that there was little he could have done for me. This was just another one of those inevitable growing pains—the "storms at sea" of which my father spoke—that we must all learn to weather. And, in the end, each of us must face those storms alone.

Chapter 17

"**B**etsy!" my mother called up from downstairs. "There's someone here to see you!"

Good heavens, I thought, *it must be Carstairs! He's finally come here to see me!* But, alas, my hair was a fright, and one hand was smeared with guava pulp. I had been drowning my sorrows in tropical fruit. *Why is it,* I wondered, *that unexpected visitors have an uncanny way of ferreting out one's most unattractive days?*

It was the morning after my row with the emperor. I was up in my room, pen in my guava-free hand, brooding on paper, as was my wont.

Carstairs! My ensign, my love, I had written. *Soon we will be reunited.*

"Coming, Mother!" I shouted, scrambling to

straighten out my hair. I wiped my sticky hand on a linen towel and cascaded downstairs with a sway and a saunter, as I imagined a London opera singer might.

"Good morning, mademoiselle."

Blast!

"Oh," I said, not bothering to conceal my enormous disappointment. "It's only you."

"Only me?" Boney replied, teasing. "That's a fine *bienvenue* for the emperor."

Poppleton stood by his side. The emperor's "nanny *du jour.*"

"Sorry," I said. Then, remembering I was supposed to still be angry with him, I added, "What do you want?"

He took me by the hand. "Come with me, mademoiselle. I am about to keep a promise I made to you."

I walked with him. It was a sticky, steamy day on St. Helena—a typically unpleasant one. It was a bit like breathing into a paper sack. Poppleton, in his tight uniform and weighed down by a heavy musket, sweated like a horse. Before long our destination became clear. Boney was taking us to Plantation House.

We rapped on the door and were admitted.

Poppleton waited outside. Reade announced us.

Governor Lowe was seated at his desk—scribbling another one of his pompous orders, I suppose. He did not bother to look up.

"So," he said facetiously. "To what do I owe the high honor of this unexpected visit?"

"This is Mademoiselle Betsy Balcombe," the emperor said. "I have learned how you have treated her family. I am not pleased with it."

"I see," Lowe said, looking up at us at last as if the effort were hardly worth the trouble. "You are not pleased. What a shame. And you have appointed yourself ambassador for this young girl? I suppose you must have something to occupy yourself, now that you won't be killing any more Englishmen." Lowe stood and poured himself a glass of water without offering any to us. "My brother was one of them, you know," he continued. "I was quite fond of him. You remember Waterloo, do you not? Oh, but of course you do."

The emperor was seething. I mentally battened down the hatches, preparing for a big typhoon.

"What right had you to confiscate and read my private correspondence!" Boney thundered. "A man's communications with his wife are inviolable, sacred—and that of the emperor of France all the more so! Only a low and common thief would deprive him of that right of connection and stain their marital bond with the foul pollution of his prying, prurient interest!"

"You don't know me, sir," Lowe replied blandly. He yawned. If the governor was perturbed, he hid it well.

"Know you?" Bonaparte said with a small, derisive laugh. He leaned on the governor's desk and practically whispered in his freckled ear: "How could I know you? Soldiers make themselves known by commanding in the field. I know the name of every English general who has distinguished himself. And I have never heard of you."

Lowe's face muscles twitched like cow haunches shooing flies. He turned bright red; and for a moment I could barely see the ugly brown stains on his face.

"I am known for doing my duty," Lowe snapped, furious.

Boney pounded his fist on the governor's desk. "So is the hangman!" Boney replied.

Lowe was speechless.

The emperor grabbed me by the hand and stormed out.

. . .

We walked—or should I say, marched at a quickstep?—back to the Briars. I could barely keep up with Boney. He must have maintained this furious pace when leading his troops on forced marches. I could tell he was still angry at the governor.

"You really shouldn't upset him so," I told the emperor.

Of course, I was secretly pleased that Boney had berated the governor. I would have liked to have done so myself. And I was flattered that the emperor had blasted him partly for my sake. But I was worried about how Lowe would treat him as a result.

"That petty quill driver!" the emperor muttered, shuffling dirt with his Moroccan slippers. "He would have me poisoned if it would mean a raise in pay!"

"Oh, I doubt he would do that," I said, hoping to reassure him.

"*Non?*" Bonaparte said, raising an eyebrow at me. "Do you recall the time he surrounded my house with his staff?"

I nodded. Marchand had told me of it.

"Never have I seen such a murderer's visage!" Boney continued. "He reminded me of those cannibals of the South Sea Islands, dancing round the prisoners whom they are going to *flambé* on the spit and devour!"

His eyes blazed like those of a wild animal who sees in the dark, and his eyebrows merged like mating caterpillars. I could not help giggling.

"What are you sniggering at, mademoiselle?

"You!" I said, laughing harder. "You look so funny when you are angry!"

Boney scowled at me. "Funny, eh? *Drôle?*"

Then the frown melted from his face. He smiled and pulled my ear—not enough to hurt. "I'll show you funny, Mademoiselle Elizabeth-We-Call-Her-Betsy Balcombe!" he said. He made a ridiculous face at me, pounded his chest, and made guttural sounds. He looked like the gorilla in Huff's laboratory. I howled.

It was good to see Boney laughing again.

That evening, I supped with the emperor and his suite.

"Marchand," he said to his valet toward the end of the meal, "this was superb. *Merveilleux!* My compliments to Le Page. Tell him I shall award him the Légion d'Honneur for that roast!"

Boney was not quite serious about the medal, of course.

"Yes, Sire," Marchand replied, heading for the kitchen.

"And bring seconds!" Boney commanded. "I am still famished!"

Yes, it was a fine meal. Having been accustomed to English cooking all my life, I was amazed by what Boney's French chef could do with a roast. My parents were dismayed that I was missing more and more meals at home.

"So, mademoiselle," Boney said mischievously. "Shall I bring *le petit* Las Cases in here? We shall pin him down for you so that you may kiss him!"

The emperor knew how much Las Cases's son repelled me, and delighted in teasing me about him.

"Oh, bring him right in!" I said facetiously, having the good sense not to get angry, as it would only encourage him.

Marchand returned from the kitchen empty-handed. He seemed rather nervous.

"Well?" the emperor said.

"*Je le regrette*, Sire," Marchand apologized uneasily. "Le Page *dit, 'Je n'en ai pas.'*"

"No meat?" Boney said, puzzled. "Why, Marchand?"

Marchand bit his lip and seemed fearful of

replying. Bertrand responded for him. "Our rations have been cut, Your Majesty. I regret to say that—"

The emperor stood up suddenly and threw his napkin on the table. "Lowe!" he thundered.

And so, for the second time that day, we paid a call on the governor. I insisted on going with him. This would be too good to miss.

Unbeknownst to Boney, some days earlier my father, in his role as purveyor, had argued vociferously against Lowe's cutting the budget for the Pavilion. But my father's pleas on the emperor's behalf had fallen on deaf ears.

Poor Poppleton was hauled away from a lucrative card game to accompany the emperor and me to Plantation House.

"You again! You are interrupting my supper!" Lowe blustered as Boney and I brushed past the orderlies and entered the dining room. "And with a dustman's manners!"

Seated at the table with him were his wife, Lady Lowe, and daughter, Charlotte, whom I'd heard was a shameless coquette. By comparison to the governor's daughter, my sister Jane was a sister in a holy order.

"Don't send me any more food!" Boney said. "I

will take my meals with those brave fellows of your Thirty-fifth Regiment over there." He pointed to the British soldiers standing guard outside, who could be seen through the window. "Not one of them will refuse to share his rations with an old fellow soldier!"

"You will take off your hat, sir, when in the presence of my wife," Lowe sneered. "And then I will thank you to get out!" Lowe turned toward the hallway. "Guards!"

The governor's orderlies rushed in and grabbed Boney by the arms.

"No!" I protested. I was sickened, too stunned to move. In his entire life I don't think anyone had dared—dared!—place his hands on the emperor like this before. These men weren't fit to lick his boots!

Though the guards carried guns and he did not, Boney courageously struggled free of them. For a small man, his strength was staggering. And, somehow, the emperor's inherent dignity discouraged them from another attempt to grab him. They stepped back.

"You have power over my body," Boney said with quiet authority, "but none over my soul. That soul is as proud, as fierce, as determined at the present moment as it was when it commanded all of Europe."

Boney shifted his gaze to a huge old tortoise—Jonathan, by name—in the corner of the room, insouciantly munching some lettuce. An incongruous sight, to be sure, the beast had been a present to the governor from the East India Company—and turtle soup had been its intended fate. But island legend had it that Lowe, animal lover that he was, had spared the old creature's hide and now it was a family pet.

"You will outlive me, Governor," the emperor remarked. "But that tortoise will outlive us both. And let us pray, for England's sake, the prince regent appoints him your successor!"

Boney turned his back on Lowe and took me by the arm. "Come, mademoiselle," he said, loud enough for all to hear. "I am in need of fresh air!"

Chapter 18

"*Chaud . . . chaud . . . plus chaud.*" The emperor guided a blindfolded Alexander with his voice as he stumbled his way around the room. Boney waited until the little boy was within inches of touching him, then danced quickly out of the way. "*Froid!* Oh, brrrrr!" the emperor said, feigning a shudder. "*Très, très froid!*"

I suppose Boney took a special interest in my little brother because his own son was about Alexander's age. He even let Alex win at the game of *colin-maillard*—very uncharacteristic of him, seeing as how the emperor hated to lose! Once Boney told me that when he was a boy his history teacher had the class line up in two groups, one under the flag of ancient Rome, the other under that of its enemy,

Carthage. Boney's big brother was assigned to the mighty former, and he to the humble latter. "Oh, how I kicked up a fuss!" Boney told me. "Wahhh! I blubbered like *un bébé*—until Teacher agreed to switch me with Joseph, so I could be on the winning side!"

The emperor finally let Alexander catch him.

"Now you're it!" Alexander crowed, handing Boney the blindfold. Boney flopped on the divan and performed a dramatic pantomime, hilariously demonstrating exhaustion.

"Please, Boney?" little Alex whined.

The emperor shrugged in mock exasperation, nodded, and took the blindfold.

Just then, Bertrand entered to announce the arrival of a letter. We all knew what it would contain. This was the day we'd been dreading for so long.

The emperor read the letter silently. He did not speak for a moment after and then rubbed his eyes and sighed.

"Well, Mademoiselle Betsy," he said, attempting to be cheerful, "it is time. What are you staring at? Send for your father."

I was too upset to do anything but obey his wishes.

"I am sorry about the shortage of provisions," my father apologized to the emperor upon entering the room. "I did my best for you, but the governor is . . . not the most amenable of fellows."

Boney waved his hand as if to say, *It is no matter.* He seemed to know that my father was not to blame.

"I thank you for all your kindness," the emperor said. "*Et vôtre femme,* your good wife, *aussi.*" He waved the letter in the air. "It seems I have a date with the rats and mildew at Longwood."

Yes, Boney knew well that his new accommodations would be a far cry from the Pavilion, but little did he know just how awful they would be.

I had visited Longwood on several occasions in the past, to get a feel for the emperor's new circumstances. The house was only five miles from the Briars, but it might have been on another world for all the two resembled each other. His new quarters sat high atop a sheer, cold cliff—one had to pass around the abyss known as the "Devil's Punchbowl" to reach it—on the most unforgivingly bleak part of St. Helena. The place was a grim volcanic wasteland under a perpetual cloud; when it wasn't raining—and it rained every day at Longwood, three times more often than elsewhere on the island—it was fogging; when not fogging, it was misting. A few pathetic sprigs of green hung tremblingly on the sheer face of that cliff—for dear life, so it seemed—but Longwood was otherwise devoid of anything resembling God's creation. A steep, heart-stoppingly narrow winding road, without rails or parapets, led up to the house. And even a sure-footed mule would be wise to get his affairs in order before attempting it.

I had chosen not to inform the emperor of my explorations of the area. What would I have told him? That the rats were so numerous, ravenous that they had skinned the few remaining gum trees like expert tanners? That the wind blew so relentlessly and cold that the inside of one's head rang with its hollow moans like a chambered nautilus? That the water was thick and fetid, would liquefy your bowels, and not fit for drinking?

And what of the house? It began life as a barn and to this day was more suited to domiciling a hog than the former emperor of a great nation. The library, facing east, stank of mold, and the room that was to be Marchand's flooded when it rained. As for the emperor's room, it was hardly large enough for a cobbler's bed, and the walls bore the hideous stains of saltpeter. Was I to have told him all this?

No, I had wisely concluded, the less the emperor knew about where he was headed, the better off he would be.

It came time to say our farewells. The rats were awaiting him.

Marchand and the others had, some days prior, packed up the emperor's belongings as well as their own. Gourgaud sat outside in the carriage.

"You must not cry, Mademoiselle Betsy," Boney said, fondly pinching my ear. "You must come and see me next week, and very often."

I nodded, choking back tears. Both of us desperately wanted to believe that we would be seeing no less of each other, that nothing had really changed. But I am certain that deep down the emperor understood as well as I that nothing, nothing would ever be the same.

Boney turned toward my father. "Balcombe, you must bring Miss Betsy to see me next week, eh? When will you ride up to Longwood?"

My father mumbled something about later in the week, but I knew that it was unlikely he would bring me with him. He thought it too dangerous a ride.

Willie was inconsolable when Boney began to

say his good-byes, so my mother was holding him on her lap, trying in vain to comfort him. Meanwhile, little Alex hugged the emperor around the waist and clung desperately to him as he walked about like a four-legged beast. When it came time to go, my brother had to be surgically removed from him by Count Montholon.

"Sire!" Gourgaud shouted impatiently from outside. "We are waiting!"

"*Un moment,* Gourgaud!" Boney shouted back.

The emperor presented me with a gift: a little candy box. "You can give it as a *gage d'amour*—a love present—to *le petit* Las Cases," he said humorously. But there was no laughter in me today.

I burst into tears and ran from the room.

From my bedroom window, I watched the emperor approach his carriage. Then I shut my eyes. It hurt my heart too much, as if a heavy boot were pressed upon it, to look upon him as he left us—and rode away.

Chapter 19

The person—more a speckled rat than a man—wore a British general's uniform and pulled a small, mounted cannon by its rope. Cackling like a demon, he chased Boney all over Longwood, whose dank hallways wound around and around like an endless maze.

Desperate to escape, the emperor ran outside the house, and the villain pursued him. They approached the edge of the chasm. There was nowhere left to run! Finally, the rat-general fired a round at Boney. But instead of cannonballs, apples emerged from the cannon. One of the apples hit Boney squarely in the face. I reached out and tried to catch him as he fell, but it was no use. He called out, "Joséphine!"—as if I were she. And with that,

Boney fell over the side of the cliff to his death.

I was weeping. And then, for some strange reason, I picked up one of the apples—the one that had killed the emperor—ate it, and spit the pips on the ground. Before my astonished eyes, the pips instantly took root, and a man, not a tree, grew from them. The man looked just like Boney! "But, no!" I said. "It cannot be you! You are dead!" He merely smiled and offered me some licorice. I said, "No, thank you; licorice is for children." And that's when I woke up.

It was no stranger than many of the dreams I'd had since returning to St. Helena, but this one stayed with me, not only because it had frightened me, but because I wondered if it contained a message. If only I could decipher it. I sat up suddenly in bed, took out a sheet of paper, and wrote down my thoughts.

Well, the evil rat-general with the speckles represented Hudson Lowe and his freckles—that was easy enough to see. And I was myself, as Joséphine. The emperor was the emperor. Clearly, my dream showed that I was worried about him. But why apples instead of cannonballs? And who was the man who looked exactly like Boney—but wasn't?

Wait! It was Roberaud. The emperor's double!

Boney had told me that Roberaud was probably in Normandy, "sitting under the apple trees." So that's where the apples in my dream came from!

Suddenly, a new idea took shape in my mind. Why didn't I think of this before? I wrote furiously:

1. *Stow away on a ship and sail to England. From there, go to France.*

2. *Find Roberaud. Try Normandy first.*

3. *Roberaud stows away on another ship and comes to St. Helena.*

4. *Roberaud hides in the wagon that brings daily provisions to Longwood.*

5. *Boney and Roberaud switch places. Boney escapes in same supply wagon. Lowe's men look through windows of Longwood—see Roberaud. Believe Boney's still there!*

6. *Boney stows away on a ship to anywhere. Arabia?*

7. *Boney conquers the world (again)!*

Yes, it was brilliant, if I do say so myself. But would Roberaud cooperate? Would he be willing to give up his freedom for the emperor's?

I had little doubt that he would. Wasn't it Boney himself who said that Roberaud was awaiting his orders? Of course, the orders would be coming from me, but surely Boney's double would understand that I was trying to help him. After all, I'd have come all the way to France to find him.

I had always known that somehow I'd find a way to free the emperor! It made me feel good to know that Huff would have been proud of me.

Now, to put my plan into effect.

"What are you writing, Betsy?" Jane sat up in bed and peered at me groggily. "A love letter?"

"Nothing, Jane. Go back to sleep."

Perhaps the best thing about my plan was that it would enable me to run away from home. To live in France! Perhaps Boney would come and visit me there, after conquering the rest of the globe.

I went downstairs and, after memorizing its contents, threw the paper outlining my plan into the fireplace. I didn't want to risk anyone finding it.

In a few days there was to be a party aboard the *Newcastle*, moored at Jamestown Harbor. It would provide a perfect opportunity for me to explore the possibilities of stowing away! It was a fete for navy men, Governor Lowe's family, and a large number of guests. None of the Balcombes were invited to the party—I suppose the governor was still angry with us—but no matter. I would mix among the guests, and no one would question my presence.

Oh, how marvelous it felt to have a purpose in life again! The emperor had been gone some weeks, and I had been in the depths of despair. I had not been permitted to see him in all that time. Had it not been for my father and Dr. O'Meara, a young, good-hearted Irishman who had Boney's confidence and kept me posted on the emperor's condition, I would have known nothing about how he fared. And by all accounts, he did not fare well. Though Lowe had appointed O'Meara physician to "the prisoner," the friendship Boney developed with his doctor came as no surprise to me. I supposed a Frenchman and an Irishman—whose countries had fought mine throughout history— could agree, if nothing else, on a mutual antipathy for anything English!

Still, it was no wonder Boney had been doing poorly in his new circumstances despite O'Meara's kindly ministrations. As soon as the emperor was installed at Longwood, the governor cracked down even harder on him. He was not permitted to speak to anyone outside his compound, nor they to him. If the prisoner happened upon a peasant while out walking or riding, he was allowed to say *bonjour*—

nothing more. Worse, his riding range had been so severely restricted that eventually the emperor refused to go out at all. For a man who had been accustomed to vigorous and lengthy daily sojourns, a sedentary lifestyle was devastating—and I feared it would have a terrible effect on his health. As I predicted, living in Longwood House was a leaden weight on Boney's spirits. It lacked not only the comforts of home, but the laughter of children.

I slipped out of the Briars unnoticed the night of the party, wearing my ball gown. The *Newcastle* was an old ship that creaked like a badly oiled rocking chair. But if she would get me to England, that was all I'd ask of her.

I'd dressed in my best so as not to call attention to myself at the fete. No one questioned or stopped me. The party was a dull but noisy sort of affair—lots of drunken, grizzled old navy men who looked like walruses and their wives and daughters—so I did not mind that I'd miss most of it.

When no one was looking, I slipped belowdecks.

I scouted around, looking for a place that a girl my size could hide. The galley was unsuitable. So was the captain's quarters, for obvious reasons. But then I saw what looked like a storage room—the perfect place for a stowaway! I tried the doorknob. What luck! It was unlocked and I opened the door.

Standing before me were two lovers locked in a passionate embrace. I don't know who was more surprised—they or I.

The lady looked up first. She screamed. Her hair was in disarray and the top of her dress was unbuttoned. It was Charlotte, the governor's daughter. Well, I can't say that part was astonishing.

"I—I'm so sorry!" I said, embarrassed. I was going to slam the door shut, but something made me hesitate. The man, who wore a military uniform and had been nuzzling Miss Lowe, came up for air.

"Carstairs!" I said.

"Betsy!" he said. "What—what are you doing here?"

"I might ask the same of you!" I replied.

"Who is this girl!?" Charlotte demanded. "How do you know her?"

The same way he knows you, dear, I thought.

"It's—it's not how it looks!" Carstairs protested. His comment seemed directed at both of us. Frantic, he tucked in his shirt. "I can explain everything!"

I was hurt, of course. Deeply. But at the moment I was more enraged than anything else. How dare he! All those flowery letters he wrote to me like the tragic French lover Abelard to his Héloïse, saying I was his one and only, and, oh, the torture of our temporary separation, and how I must, I must be strong! And now this—and with that tramp, of all people!

"Charlotte, my dear," Carstairs said, taking her by the hand. "I think you had better leave us for a moment while I take care of this."

"This," I suppose, meant me. How degrading!

Carstairs led a vociferously protesting Charlotte to one of the cabins and closed the door. Then he returned to where I was standing glowering at him.

"Well?" I said. Carstairs shifted nervously from one foot to the other.

"Betsy, you must understand," he began lamely. "Your father would never have approved of us. Charlotte is older than you, a different sort of girl . . ."

"So I've noticed," I replied.

"That's not what I mean! Betsy, I—"

"Courting—if you call that courting!—the daughter of the governor can have certain advantages for a young sailor in search of a promotion," I snapped.

"Me? What about you!" Carstairs said acidly. His handsome face looked very ugly indeed. How could I ever have thought him attractive? "It seems to me, Miss Balcombe, you're not above offering yourself up to the right sort of people for personal gain. Tell me, my dear innocent: What did you have to do for General Bonaparte to get that diamond necklace you were wearing at the admiral's farewell ball?"

I slapped him. I was not in the habit of striking people, but special circumstances call for special adjustments. Carstairs turned on his heel and stomped off. I stood there for a few moments alone, nursing my broken heart. My hand stung. I had no idea it actually hurt the perpetrator to hit someone and vowed not to do it again.

As I headed for the stairs leading to the deck, I suddenly remembered what Carstairs had forgotten: Charlotte was still waiting for him in the ship's cabin. The hussy! I noticed a silver key in the lock outside the cabin door. God help me, but I couldn't resist. I turned the key and pocketed it.

Back on deck, no one was the wiser. If Charlotte was yelling to get out, as I'm quite certain she was, nobody could hear her over the party noise and ship's creaking. Carstairs had left the party. Not long after, I went home. I subsequently learned that it was only some hours later that Carstairs remembered where he had left Charlotte. And since she hadn't contacted him, he'd merely assumed that she was still angry over the incident with me and would find him in due course.

It was the boatswain on the *Newcastle* who eventually found Charlotte. They had to break the door down to get her out. The girl looked a fright, so I was told. She never knew how she had gotten locked into that cabin. Charlotte, rather short on brains, must have believed she had somehow done it herself—or that Carstairs had—and was too embarrassed to tell anyone. Of course, she didn't want to explain what she was doing belowdecks on the *Newcastle* to begin with. And here was the best thing of all: The captain of the ship accused her of being a stowaway! This caused great embarrassment for her father, Hudson Lowe, and great pleasure for me. Too bad the emperor wasn't there to see it!

I barely had time to savor my victory when I received some very troubling news the morning after the party. Hudson Lowe's latest orders were posted to trees here and there on the island. From that day forth, all ships leaving St. Helena were to be thoroughly searched by the governor's aides before being permitted to set sail. No doubt his daughter's misfortune on the *Newcastle*, as well as a desire for stricter security, helped prompt this decision.

Blast! Now it would be impossible for me to stow away! By indulging in a harmless prank, I had inadvertently sealed my own fate.

And with a sudden, crashing sense of defeat, I understood the full impact of this state of affairs. I would *never* be able to help the emperor escape! He would never again bask in the glory of conquering nations, never again bring freedom to the masses. Oh, it was all so undeniably, unbearably true! Napoleon Bonaparte was going to live out his remaining years and die right here—on this miserable wart on the face of the deep. And it was all my fault!

Chapter 20

St. Helena stays virtually the same from season to season. Against this never-changing backdrop, the changing scene of life is so much easier to notice. If you stand before the looking glass, you can almost watch your hair grow. And looking at myself in the year and more since the emperor had been deported to Longwood, I saw a girl I hardly knew. My hair was blonder than it had been when bathed in London fog, and my eyes were bluer—as if mirroring the sea. My cheeks were less cherubically round, but the rest of me was rounder—quite pleasingly so. In the regions of the heart I had changed even more— and more disturbingly. Where once dwelled the conviction that all things were possible, lovers were true, England righteous, and soldiers brave, there now lived a sadder knowledge. And its most painful recognition was that Betsy Balcombe was no longer a carefree girl—and not, by God, invincible.

I was able to see the emperor only once during all that time—in deference to my father's wishes. I suppose now that I was older, those wishes were not as easy for me to ignore as they had been when I had first returned to the island. But I missed the emperor mightily.

Countess Montholon had a baby. Dr. O'Meara told me of it, since he had officiated at her lying-in. Madame claimed the little girl had her father's "taste for licorice." So it was no surprise to anyone that she named her Napoleone. The emperor once told me there is neither happiness nor unhappiness. The life of a happy man is a picture showing black stars on a silver background. The life of an unhappy man is a picture of silver stars on black. Optimistic as he was by nature, I had little doubt that the birth of this child, this blessed event, was the one bright star in the emperor's sky of pitch.

My mother warned me not to see Boney anymore. The governor objected, she said. Didn't I understand I was endangering my future? she said. And, what's more, I was jeopardizing my father's position, she said.

Painful as it was for me now to disregard my parents' wishes, one day I determined that it was neccessary for me to do just that. It was now 1817 I'd had no news of the emperor for some time and wanted to see him for myself. Napoleone or no Napoleone, Boney needed me now more than ever—and I was no fair-weather friend!

But as was often the case with my best-laid plans, Hudson Lowe set them awry. I awoke the next morning to find copies of the governor's latest order bored into every tree like maggots. Henceforth and effective immediately, no one was allowed to see the prisoner without a pass. And any pass would be issued at the sole discretion of His Excellency Lieutenant General Sir Hudson Lowe, K.C.B., etc., etc.

At my urging—or, more to the point, my tearful pleading, whining, and cajoling—my father went to the governor to request a pass for his younger daughter. But the request was summarily denied.

For the moment, and only for the moment, I put my plans to see Boney on hold.

From time to time in the months that followed Dr. O'Meara would do me the favor of examining Belle's leg. It had been fine since shortly after my return to St. Helena, but this gave me an excuse to see the doctor and ask about Boney. No one was suspicious of these meetings since there were no animal doctors on the island.

On one of these visits to the barn, O'Meara brought me some disturbing news. "He's ill, lass," the doctor said in his soft-spoken brogue. He shook his head sadly. "Though it'd not be surprising me, with all the governor's harsh ways."

"The emperor ill?" I said, frightened. "What is the trouble with him?"

The good doctor shrugged. "A man of medicine would point to his stomach. Aye, a man of the cloth would say it's his soul. But between you and me, dearie, I believe it's his spirit. And when a man's spirit is what ails him, there's no medicine strong enough for it. More's the pity. . . ."

I was stunned. Boney was strong, vital—younger than I, in many ways. How could he possibly be unwell? Still, I knew the doctor had told me the truth. I sat down on the straw next to Belle and tried to absorb the shock of the doctor's words.

"Will you take me to see him?"

O'Meara shook his head. "I wish I could help you, lass," he said. "By God, I wish I could. It would do the emp a world of good too, no denying. But if I cross that cocky Englishman, he'll have my head on a platter. And heaven only knows the

London butcher they'll bring in to replace me."

I realized the doctor was right. As long as O'Meara was Boney's physician, I knew he'd be in the best of hands. But who knew what evil deeds the doctor's successor, handpicked by Lowe, might do at the governor's bidding? We couldn't risk it.

I thanked O'Meara, and he went on his way. I stayed in the barn a while longer, currying Belle. It was nightfall. And right then and there I made up my mind.

"Shall you take me for a ride tonight, girl?" I said to her. "To see our old friend, Boney? Shall you? It will be dangerous, I want you to know. Armed sentries everywhere. You can always refuse if that worries you. . . ."

But Belle did not fail me.

It was a warm, muggy night, the sort that made me long for a whiff of London and the river Thames. Burly mosquitoes—so impressive that they must have had distant relations in the elephant family—swarmed ravenously about my face. Belle kept her mind on the road. For that I was grateful, since navigating the steep, death-defying path up to Longwood required the meticulous concentration of a biblical scholar. Once or twice Belle slipped a bit and I got a view of the Devil's Punchbowl that gin and orange slices might envy. But for the most part, this part of our trip was clear sailing.

Then came the difficult part. *Blast!* Lowe's troops were camped all around Longwood: soldiers by the hundreds—asleep but ready to spring into action at the slightest sound—cannon to the right of us, cannon to the left of us. I scanned the governor's arsenal, hoping to find a gap between the lines. At last I found a thin spot, if not a gap, where a few soldiers were sprawled out on the ground, snoring loudly. I saw the shadow of one soldier, sitting in a tent. He was singing a song tipsily—a ditty of the sort one doesn't repeat in polite company.

Longwood lay just beyond these men. If I could just sneak past them . . .

Riding would be too noisy. I dismounted and, leading Belle by the halter, tiptoed past the sleeping soldiers.

"Mary, Mary darling!" one man called out. He was close enough for me to smell the liquor on his breath. The man rolled back and forth fitfully, and I realized he was talking in his sleep. That set my mind at ease. Until . . .

"Mary, is that you?" the soldier said in a dream

state. Sleepily, he sat up and grabbed hold of my ankle!

"Yes, darling," I said. "I'm here. Now go back to sleep." I stooped and patted him on the cheek.

Eyes still shut, the man smiled blissfully, like a baby. I waited, hardly daring to breathe, until he rolled over and his hand loosed its grip on my leg. Carefully, I slipped my ankle out of his grasp. He had never been awake, but I did not feel reassured until I heard the slow, steady rhythm of his snoring once more.

Belle and I crept on. Longwood was only a few dozen yards away. Here at last! I rejoiced at the thought of how glad Boney would be to see me. After hiding Belle behind the barn, I rapped quietly on Longwood's front door.

It was sleepy Marchand who answered it. "Mademoiselle!" He was clearly astonished to see me. He yawned. "What time is it?"

"Long past time," I said. "I am here to see the emperor."

"He's asleep. He's . . . very ill, mademoiselle."

I nodded. "Yes, I know," I replied. "That's why I've come."

The young man hesitated, troubled.

"Please, Marchand!" I said. "I have come all

this way just to see him. It was very dangerous, and—"

"All right, Betsy," he said, motioning for me to come inside. *"Un moment. . . ."*

Marchand went to wake the emperor and inform him of my presence. He returned quickly to me. "Be brief," he admonished.

Marchand led me through the damp rooms of Longwood to the darkness of the emperor's bedside. He whispered in my ear before he left me with my old friend: "Prepare yourself."

But what—what on earth—could possibly prepare me for the horrible sight that met my eyes? I lit the lamp, and there, propped up on pillows in bed, was a man who might have been a distant cousin to the one I once knew. His skin was a sickening yellow, like a tallow; his face, bloated and puffy. Though it was quite chilly up here on the Longwood plateau, beads of perspiration dripped from the emperor's forehead. The bedsheets were stained dark with it. He coughed—a terrible, hollow sound that shall reverberate in my memory forever. I silently berated myself for not having found a way to come see him sooner.

He spoke and his voice was strong—just the same as always. "I have just seen my good Joséphine. I reached out my arms to her, but she would not embrace me! She slipped away the moment I wanted to hold her in my arms." He pointed a trembling finger to a corner of the room. "She was sitting there." I followed his gaze and saw nothing but an empty chair. "She hadn't changed—always the same, still completely devoted to me. Joséphine told me we were going to see each other again and never part. She has promised me! Did you see her?"

His words shook me no less than his other-worldly appearance. I swallowed and screwed up my courage. "No, Boney," I said. "I—I did not."

He stared at me. "Why are you here?" he demanded angrily. "Who said you could come to see me!"

I was stunned and frightened by his sudden outburst. Perhaps it was only his illness talking, but it scared me just the same.

"I . . . wanted to see you," I replied. "I thought you would want to see me."

The emperor trembled—with fever or rage, I could not be certain.

"No!" he said. "You presume too much. You are not my friend, mademoiselle! You can no longer help me to escape. It is very simple. I like only those people who are useful to me, and only so long as they are useful!"

I could not have been more hurt if he'd struck me in the face with a hammer. What had happened to him? Could it be that he had never really cared for me? Was I merely an instrument of his designs, a stupid little fool? No! It could not be!

"But—but I thought—"

"You thought wrong, mademoiselle! Call this a good lesson in life. You will have more of them." He wiped his sweaty face with a towel.

I stood there at his bedside, too stricken to speak. Devolving into a whirlpool, spinning in another nightmare—but this time my dream was for real.

Boney coughed a few more times. "Marchand!" he called out.

"Yes, Sire," the young man replied, entering the room. "Are you all right?"

"Show the young lady to the door."

The emperor turned his attention back to me. "You shall not be welcome here again!" he said savagely.

And with that, the emperor—or whatever demon had taken over his soul—blew out the lamp.

Chapter 21

First Carstairs, now the emperor! There must be something poisonous in the air on St. Helena. *Step right up, ladies and gents, and take a whiff of some Bona Fide Tropical Atmosphere—fresh off the boat from hell! Hurry, hurry, hurry! She's fetid, she wriggles into your moral fiber, she corrupts. Here—take a whiff, sir. Breathe her in and sell your soul to the devil!*

Was anything what it seemed? A friend was a foe. A lover, a louse. My nightmares seemed real; my life, like a nightmare. Was anything real? Was I?

Anger burned in my throat like bile. Boney was a lying scoundrel, and I had been foolish enough to be taken in by his oily charm! I fancied myself all grown up, and, in fact, I had been a stupid, gullible child. Well, I suppose I wasn't the first to be deceived by the emperor of France. Hadn't he himself once told me, "You are not a very good liar. . . . Never mind. I have had more practice at it than you"?

Belle and I made it back from Longwood without any difficulty. I suspect part of me had been secretly hoping the sentries would discover us. After all, what had I to live for? The two most important people in the world to me had casually thrown me over, like so much offal tossed out a kitchen window.

"Well, Belle," I said, tucking her in for the night, "it looks like it's just you and me now."

Usually, a good night's sleep made me feel like a new girl. But when day dawned, I felt as melancholy as ever. So I visited Belle. I still planned to run her in the Deadwood Races later that week, as had been my plan ever since my return from Miss Hawthorne's school. But, in truth, my heart was not in it.

"Dr. O'Meara!" I called out as he was passing by the barn on his way to calling on my father.

"What is it, lass?"

"Would you take a look at Belle? I want to make sure she's sound for the race."

O'Meara obliged me, singing merrily at his work. He tapped Belle's knee gently with a silver instrument from his bag.

"*Janet kilts her green kirtle*
A little aboon her knee,
And she has snood her yellow hair
A little aboon her bree,
And she is to her father's ha,
As fast as she can hie! . . ."

I wondered whether the good doctor was flirting with me. And that silly burr he sang in to amuse me—pretending to be a Scotsman, no less! Though my heart was heavy, I was touched by the doctor's kind and gentle smile.

"Right as rain," he said, returning Belle's hoof to the stable floor, "and ready to romp." He studied me. A serious look came over him. "What's the matter, dearie? Sure, you look like your leprechaun's run out on you and taken his crock of gold."

"Nothing, really," I said. "But it is kind of you to ask."

He did not press me. The doctor patted Belle on the flanks and sighed. "Ah, 'tis a pity that Englishman doesn't treat humans half as well as horseflesh," he said sadly. I was sure O'Meara was referring to Lowe's abuse of the emperor—and of the doctor himself, no doubt. "Lass, you should see the gov with his own nag, Lord Nelson. Oh, the primin' and the pamperin'! Says he wants him shipshape for the Deadwood Races. Aye, he dotes on that beast like a pretty colleen!"

The doctor tweaked my nose playfully. "There, you've given me a smile, lass. Don't shock me now, dearie!"

I laughed. He winked at me.

"I must be going on my way," O'Meara said, shutting his bag of instruments. "Your da's expecting me." He waved good-bye. "Keep that smile in a safe place now, where you can find it for me!"

I waved back, feeling grateful for his high spirits. Cheerfulness was certainly in short supply in this dreary place.

"Any message for the emp?" O'Meara called over his shoulder. "I'll be seeing him right soon."

A new wave of rage at Boney washed over me. "No. No message."

"Sure now, lass? He's been feeling poorly."

"The emperor has no use for me," I said firmly. "So I have none for him."

A baffled look on his face, O'Meara walked back toward me. "No use for you?" He crossed his arms. "Now, where for the love of Mike did you get a fool notion such as that?"

"It's not a fool notion!" I said. "He told me so."

O'Meara sat down on a bale of hay and shook his head in disbelief. "How on earth did you get to see him?"

"It wasn't easy," I replied.

"You shouldn't have risked it. You might have gotten yourself killed!"

"I know, and it wasn't worth it. He didn't want to see me anyway."

O'Meara shrugged. "You must be misunderstandin' the man, lass," he said. "He speaks of you all the time! Hardly a day goes by . . ." O'Meara then did a fair imitation of Boney: "'What? Bah— medicine again! If only Betsy were here, Docteur! I would never again have to look upon your lugubriously concerned countenance and swallow your vile calomel!'"

Yes, that did indeed sound like Boney. At least, the Boney I once knew. The doctor was clearly not making it up in order to assuage my feelings.

"But . . . I don't understand," I said. "When I saw him he acted like . . . well, as if he hated me!"

"Poor Betsy." O'Meara put his hand on my shoulder. "I fear he's put one over on you, lass. A bit of an actor, he is, your friend Boney."

"But, why? Why would he—say such terrible things to me and not mean them?"

"I know you must have risked your hide by going to see him," O'Meara explained. "Aye? Well, he knows that too. The emperor doesn't want you putting your life on the line for his sake."

"Are you sure?"

The doctor nodded. "He was just protecting you, dearie. And your family. That's why, and no mistaking. I'd bet my life on it."

O'Meara bade me good-bye and promised to call again.

If I'd felt stupid when I woke up this morning, I felt like a perfect idiot now. The doctor's theory about Boney made perfect sense. The emperor had only been thinking about what was best for me and my family! He knew I would never have agreed to desert him of my own accord—not even if he pleaded with me to. So Boney stopped me from visiting him the only way he knew how: by making me hate him! How could I have failed to figure this out myself?

Betsy, old girl, you will have to learn from this experience, I vowed, *and not turn on your friends so easily again.*

"Why didn't you tell me, Belle?" I said, rubbing her cheek. "Oh, why didn't you tell me what a fool I've been?" I gave her a nibble of a lump of sugar.

"Well, I suppose it's not your fault," I said. "I'm supposed to be grown up enough to figure these things out for myself. . . . Shall you run a fine race for me on Saturday? Yes? There's a good girl. You know, I've had a terrible row with our friend Boney. He's quite ill, I'm afraid. Oh, he looks a pitiful sight! Have I told you?"

Belle seemed to nod.

"Yes," I said. "It's quite serious. How I wish—how I wish there was something—anything!—I could do to help him. If only there was some hope!"

Belle whinnied and stamped her hoof. She suddenly reared up on her hind legs, and it took all my strength to hold her.

"Easy, girl, easy! What is it?" Belle's glorious head nearly grazed the roof of the barn.

And all of a sudden, I understood what she was trying to tell me. *Of course! That's it!* I thought. *A plan to help Boney!*

"By God, Belle, you're brilliant! You know, I think it just may actually work. It's daring, it's outrageous, but—it just—might—work."

Belle settled down. And I set to work.

"Dr. O'Meara!" I called out, looking for him at the Briars. He was just finishing up treating my father's gout.

"You're looking cheerier, lass," he said.

I grabbed him by the hand and spoke in an earnest whisper: "I must speak with you!"

It seemed everyone on St. Helena—from blacksmith to boatswain, from cook to cobbler to captain—had come to this place dressed in their churchgoing best. Even the slaves were permitted to lay down their hoes and watch the Deadwood Races from a separate section of the viewing stands. It was early September 1817, and this was going to be the most important day of my life.

The Union Jack rippled in the breeze, snapping crisply like a topgallant sail on the mainmast. Ladies wore short white gloves and wide-brimmed hats as big as platters for Yorkshire pudding— flouncing about as if they fancied themselves at the Ascot Races on opening day. The women competed desperately with one another for the young officers' attention. To me, it was a bit like watching rats fight over a piece of Stilton cheese.

Governor Lowe and his family were sitting in a roped-off section of the stands. It was a sweltering day. A perspiring slave, the governor's personal "property," waved a large, fanlike object at Mrs. Lowe. It beat slowly back and forth, back and forth,

like the flapping of an elephant's ears. Was there anything more lazy than a woman too shiftless to wave her
own hand to keep herself cool? Charlotte sat to the
governor's right; she was showing enough white flesh
above the top of her skimpy dress to blind a desert
chieftain. As for Lowe himself, he had a smile on his
face like the cat that swallowed a canary. *With a little
luck*, I thought, *he'll soon be gagging on feathers.*

I scanned the viewing stands for a glimpse of my
family. I knew that they were up there, somewhere.

Thomas Reade, Lowe's assistant and now also
the chief of police on St. Helena, had volunteered to
announce the race. There were six horses running.
Had it been held in England, the race would have
been described as a mile-and-an-eighth on the
turf for three-year-olds and up, six starters, two
fillies, four colts, no weight limit. But on St. Helena
we were much less formal.

"Tenth running of the Deadwood Races shall
begin!" Reade announced. One of the soldiers blew
a bugle—far too close to my ear, I'm afraid—and the
jockeys brought the horses on parade. Gambling
was supposed to be strictly prohibited on St.
Helena, but it was actually quite common here and
island officials turned a blind eye to it, especially
on race day. I had it on O'Meara's authority that Sir

Hudson Lowe had put one thousand pounds on his Lord Nelson to win. All "under the table," of course. Where the man got that kind of money, I'll never know. Probably skimming funds from the budget for Longwood.

"Number six, Northern Lights," Reade announced as a bay filly paraded in front of the crowd. "Robert Tappen aboard." The jockey tipped his hat to the crowd, and they applauded loudly. I knew Tappen, of course. He was a local favorite. Tappen was a good rider, and Northern Lights always had a strong kick left after the final post.

"Number five, Hampton Court," Reade called out. "Ridden by Calville Boland." I didn't know Boland, but I knew the horse. Hampton Court had won the Deadwood Races last year but was coming back from a leg injury and might not be up to par. He tended to run off the pace, though, so the race might set up just right for him.

"Number four, Star of India," said Reade. "Jockey is Angus McCartland." A Scottish jockey on a Bengali horse—talk about strange bedfellows! "Number three, Catherine of Aragon, ridden by Captain James Henry." That was the other filly in the race. It had rained earlier that morning; that was a plus for her—she ran well on an off track. I'd seen her in her workouts last spring, and no doubt about it, Catherine could be dangerous in the mud.

"Number two, Old King George," Reade announced. "Jockey is—" Someone tapped Reade on the shoulder and whispered in his ear. He nodded. "Er . . . pardon me," Reade said. "Correction: Number two has been scratched. Repeat: Old King George will not be starting!"

There were a few boos from the crowd. I guess somebody had put money on him.

And then Governor Lowe's pampered prince high-stepped onto the track accompanied by a lead pony with a braided mane. Lowe's horse had the same obnoxious hauteur of his master.

"Number one, Lord Nelson!" Reade called out. Charlotte squealed loudly, and she and her mother—as well as Lowe's numerous cronies—cheered so raucously for the governor's horse that they drowned out Reade's voice and I couldn't hear the jockey's name. Ah, well. No matter. It was time for me to swing into action.

I ran up to Reade and whispered to him.

"We have a last-minute entry," he announced to the crowd. "Miss Betsy Balcombe, on her horse—" He broke off and turned toward me. "What's the name of your mount, miss?"

But I had already left him to retrieve my horse from behind the viewing stands and mount up. The other entries were now positioned at the starting line, and the man who'd blown the bugle held a starter's pistol aloft. They—and the noisy restless crowd—were all awaiting my return. I brought my horse onto the track.

A collective gasp came from the crowd.

Well, in truth, they could hardly be blamed. For my horse that day was not Belle, but Napoleon Bonaparte's Hope! There was no mistaking who owned this magnificent creature: From head to pastern, he was decked out in imperial tack. Red velvet trappings were emblazoned with the Golden Bees—known around the world as symbolic of Napoleon's reign—and the initials "NB" were scripted beautifully beneath them, writ so large that even old King George could have read them without his spectacles.

I tied on a blue bonnet, and the picture was complete. Between us, Hope and I wore all the hues of the French flag: the blue, white, and red of the tricolor!

Good Dr. O'Meara had smuggled Hope out of Longwood with the horse's livery rolled up tightly and hidden in his medicine bags. All this was done with Boney's blessing, and I knew that at this very moment the emperor was peering down from the Longwood plateau through the spyglass that had served him at Austerlitz—seeing everything as clear as the cloudless blue sky over me and anxiously awaiting the start of the race.

Then the crowd surprised me. They applauded!— first just a few brave souls, then the sound grew louder and bolder when they were joined by others. Apparently, the emperor had more friends on St. Helena than I had ever imagined.

Of course, one man was not applauding. A quick glance up into the stands told me that Governor Lowe was already on his feet and apoplectic with rage. He was shouting something to his aides and waving his arms. Within seconds, a phalanx of armed soldiers was headed in my direction. *Blast! Are they going to yank me off the track?*

The soldiers came at me furiously, muskets raised, their coats a red blur.

And then Dr. O'Meara, God bless him, took matters into his own hands. He grabbed the starter's pistol from the very perplexed man who held it and fired a shot!

We were off!

And for the next two minutes or so, with five

thousand pounds of horseflesh pounding furiously around the racecourse, even the king himself would not have been able to stop us.

Star of India broke first, setting a fast pace. Lord Nelson had the rail—Hope and I, to his right. The inside post gave Nelson an advantage—a shorter trip around the course. The track was still wet; mud spattered in every direction. Hope broke alertly and was eager to run, but I rated him, saving ground for later. Leaning forward, I whispered into his ear, "Boney's counting on you, old boy. He's counting on us. I know you won't let us down!"

I glanced over my shoulder. Catherine of Aragon was gaining fast, coming up between horses. The mud suited her, just as I'd feared. Oh no! She passed us!

We rounded the first turn; the crowd grew more vociferous: "Come on, Catherine!" a man shouted. "Show them the way!"

Hope and I were neck and neck with Boland on Hampton Court, two lengths off the pace. Catherine was now on the lead, with Lord Nelson half a length behind me. My hair whipped my cheeks; my knuckles turned white, a death grip on the reins.

Star of India, the speed horse, ran out of steam and dropped back like a rock. Boland made his move, coming up fast on the outside. I asked Hope for some speed. Tappen on Northern Lights moved up, held steady, hoping we'd burn up in a speed duel and he'd pick up the pieces.

Then, thundering hooves coming up on the inside. Flashing, pounding, it was Lord Nelson, driving hard! Tearing down the backstretch—holy mother-of-pearl! The jockey riding him—Carstairs!

That traitor! I might have known.

"Go, Nelson! Give 'em the boot!" came a cry from the stands. I'd swear it was Charlotte's squeals I heard. Mud in my nose, mud in my eyes, my mouth—Nelson and Hope battled for the lead. Only a furlong to go. *Hang on, Hope!*

Carstairs lowered his crop to the side. What was he up to? I lurched forward. Damn the cheating scoundrel! He'd tripped my horse! Hope bobbled, stumbled. "Steady, boy!"

Nelson took the lead!

Hope veered wide. "Steady!" I got him under control. Brave as his master, hadn't he faced worse than this? Battles and cannons and rockets! We were back on course. I gave him the spurs. *Make them eat mud, boy. Vive la France!*

Hope came alive, blazing like a comet, shooting past the final pole, burning for revenge! Burning up the track. Chasing Nelson down the stretch! *Come on, Hope! Do it for Boney!*

The crowd was on its feet, roaring, screaming.

"Go do it, Hope!" came from the stands. What fearless bloke was that?

Tappen challenged briefly but faded fast under pressure. It was Hope and Nelson, Hope and Nelson. Now drawing away. Neck and neck, nostril to nostril, eyebrow to eyebrow! Here comes the wire!

I shut my eyes, leaning forward with all my might. And we crossed the finish line.

When I opened my eyes, people were swarming about us. Someone had placed a ring of roses around Hope's neck.

By Jove, we'd done it! I—that is, we—that is, the emperor had won! There I was, looking like a charwoman, wiping the mud from my cheeks.

Lowe was livid, on his feet. Yelling something about "disqualification." But the crowd was shouting, cheering. We Brits like to see the mighty fallen. Lowe had made a lot of enemies since arriving on St. Helena, and no one gave a brass farthing what the silly gov had to say.

Well, well! Well, well, indeed. How do you like the taste of canary feathers, Sir Hudson Lowe?

Chapter 22

My poor father. When he summoned me later that day at the Briars, he didn't seem able to make up his mind whether he was more angry with me or proud for what I'd done at Deadwood. So he sentenced me to thirty minutes' confinement in my room—the briefest imprisonment of my criminal career.

Governor Lowe, I'm sorry to say, was not similarly lenient with my father. He fired him from his position as purveyor of Longwood, and Lowe said he'd send a scathing report to the East India Company—a missive that we all knew was virtually certain to cost my father his other position as superintendent of public sales as well. I was wracked by guilt, for strange as it sounds, it had not occurred to me that the governor would punish my father for my doings.

As for the emperor, I got a detailed account through O'Meara about his reaction to the race. It seems that when Boney watched the stretch run through his spyglass, he couldn't see well enough to know which horse had gone under the wire first. Desperate to learn the outcome, Boney had practically tackled O'Meara when the doctor arrived back at Longwood some hours later.

"Well? Well?" the emperor had demanded.

"It was Betsy on Hope!" O'Meara told him, dancing a jig and raising his fist in the air. "By a head, to be sure, but the lass won it!"

Boney kissed the doctor on both cheeks. "*Formidable!* I knew it. I knew it!" he crowed. The emperor sat down, exhausted from the effort of standing, savoring his victory. "Ah!" he said. "The corpse of an enemy always smells sweet."

"Rest easy, my lad," O'Meara said, patting him on the shoulder. "We'll be wanting you alive to see other happy days."

The doctor told me that it was the first time he'd seen the emperor smile in months. "And you know what else the man said, dearie?" O'Meara asked me eagerly. I shook my head. He imitated Boney's pinched accent: "'*Eh bien,* this almost makes up for my defeat by Wellington, *n'est-ce pas,* Docteur?'"

What joy, what rapture! It was I, Betsy Balcombe, who had given the emperor of France his last victory.

But in the meantime, my father was going down to defeat. And I was determined to do something about it.

"Miss Elizabeth Balcombe," Reade announced me to the governor. I stepped into the office, where Lowe was stooped over, feeding a guava to Jonathan the tortoise. Perhaps Lord Nelson was no longer his favorite pet.

The governor looked bilious at the mere sight of me.

"Sir," I blurted out. "My father knew nothing of my ride on Hope. He doesn't know I'm here. But I came to tell you it was not his fault and if you are displeased with anyone it must be with me."

"I am glad you are here, Miss Balcombe," Lowe replied sharply. "You shall save me the trouble of having to make a trip to the Briars to convey a message to your father. Tell him that the Balcombes are to be deported from St. Helena at the orders of Sir Hudson Lowe."

Deported? Booted off St. Helena like common criminals?

"What?" I said. "You—you can't do that!"

"I assure you, Miss Balcombe," he replied calmly, feeding another juicy tidbit to the tortoise, "I can and I will. You have been fraternizing with the prisoner, disturbing the peace, associating with an enemy of the Crown. You and your family represent a threat to security, and I have been given the authority to do whatever I deem necessary to preserve it. Young woman, consider yourself fortunate I don't have you hanged for treason! You are dismissed."

Words of contempt bubbled up from my core. There was no use holding back now. After all, what more trouble could I possibly get myself into? I gritted my teeth in disgust.

"You—you—" I struggled to think of a worthy name to call him. I tried one of Boney's. "You petty quill driver!"

Well. That certainly felt good.

"That will be all, Miss Balcombe," Lowe replied, ignoring the insult. He sat down at his desk and scribbled on a ledger.

I turned to go. And then it dawned on me. I was never, never going to see Boney again. I had to see him again. I had to!

"Um . . . Governor Lowe?"

"What is it now?" he snapped.

With what I was about to ask him, I was suddenly very sorry that I hadn't stopped myself from calling him a quill driver. "May I see him before we go? Just once?"

He stared at me, no doubt relishing my groveling.

"Please, sir?" I said.

Lowe crossed his arms and smiled that death's head smile of his. "Never let it be said that I am not a generous man," he said at last. "Yes, you can see your charming playmate, Miss Balcombe. One time only—on the very day you leave St. Helena. That is all. Is that clear?"

"Yes, sir," I said.

As I walked out the door, I suppressed an almost uncontrollable urge to vomit.

My father would have fought our eviction from St. Helena, but my mother was developing rheumatism and he felt a change in climate would be the best thing for her.

It was no small task to move a lifetime of possessions off of a remote island in the South Atlantic. There were Alex's toys and Willie's books, my father's souvenirs from his sailing days, and all the useless nonsenses my mother had collected over the years and couldn't bear to leave behind. Even a humble baby's bowl uncovered from some dusty cupboard made my mother dissolve into a puddle of tears, which seriously slowed our departure. I had little of my own to pack; I always travel lightly, poised for quick getaways, I suppose. But Jane's dresses alone could have filled a freighter!

Christmas came, but without the usual joy of the season. In hopes of bringing us better luck in the year to come, my mother defied her aching hands and baked mince pies, which, so tradition had it, promised a month of happiness for each one eaten. Then my father lighted the Yule log with a stick saved from last year's fire—supposedly to protect the house from burning down after our departure. But when the mince pies quickly turned rancid from St. Helena's damp climate and the Yule log failed to "catch" on the first try, even my optimistic mother had to acknowledge that this did not bode well for us.

As we gathered dutifully round Willie's piano to sing "Auld Lang Syne" for our last New Year's Eve on St. Helena, my thoughts wandered to someone I knew well, who also had little to celebrate. The clock struck midnight, and I wondered, what was he

doing, what was he thinking, at this very moment?
I found new meaning in the song's words:

> *Should auld acquaintance be forgot*
> *and never brought to mind?*
> *Should auld acquaintance be forgot*
> *and days of auld lang syne?*
> *And here's a hand, my trusty friend*
> *And gie's a hand o' thine*
> *We'll tak' a cup o' kindness yet*
> *For days of auld lang syne.*

The sad days stretched into weeks, then months, as we made final preparations for our departure. I noticed our packing seemed to go ever more slowly as the day we all hoped would never come drew near.

All in all, it wasn't until March of 1818 that my father affixed a padlock to the front door of the Briars. Though I pleaded with them tearfully, my parents would not permit me to take Belle with us back to London. The captain had told them there was no room on the ship for swine. Imagine!—calling a horse such as Belle "swine"! It pained me awfully to leave her behind, but I took some consolation from knowing that I had left her in Toby's tender care.

The trunks and boxes were waiting, and all that remained was for me to say farewell to my friends. Toby and I embraced silently; we had known each other too long and loved each other too well for mere words. At my insistence, my father had finally granted Toby his freedom; and he and Belle would be bound for Haiti, the land of his birth, on the next boat out of Jamestown. I hoped with all my heart that both of them would find peace and happiness there.

At last, it was time for me to pay my most important call, and I insisted I make it alone.

I found the emperor sitting in his garden at Longwood, reading a book. His health had improved considerably since the Deadwood Races, but Dr. O'Meara had warned me that his illness had peaks and valleys—much like St. Helena herself— and that the prognosis for his eventual recovery was not good.

Boney had done wonders with that garden. Everywhere one looked were flowers—blue, white, and red, of course—all trying to outdo one another in magnificence for the emperor's pleasure. The small plot of hardscrabble land in front of Longwood was now a greenery of which the ancient biblical city of Babylon could be proud.

"Ah, mademoiselle," Boney said as if he'd last

seen me only yesterday. "'Come into my parlor,' said the spider to the fly. Don't worry, Betsy, I won't bite."

"You did last time," I said with a smile.

"That is true," he said. He swept off his hat and made a small bow. *"Pardonnez-moi."*

He was looking much better than when I had seen him last. I sat down next to him in a wicker chair and inhaled the sweet fragrance of the flowers.

"I like your garden," I said.

"Merci, mademoiselle. It is an earthly paradise, which I shall soon exchange for the real thing."

"You must not talk like that! You frighten me."

Boney shrugged. He opened to a page of his book and read:

> *"But she was in this world where beauty*
> *Has the harshest fate;*
> *A rose, she lived the life that roses live,*
> *A morning's space."*

"Very pretty," I said. "Did you write that?"

"In war and literature," Boney replied, "I always give credit where credit is due. *C'est* François de Malherbe, not I."

The emperor gazed off into the distance, to the mountains and the sea. Clouds ringed the towering peaks, as if God had been playing horseshoes.

"You will be sailing over the rim of the sea toward England," he said sadly, "while I stay to die on this miserable rock. Look at these mountains, Betsy! These are my prison walls. Soon, you will hear the Emperor Napoleon is dead."

Until now I had retained the illusion that we would see each other again. But the charade was over. The dam broke, and I wept.

I fished in my dress pocket for my handkerchief—and realized I'd already packed it up in my trunk.

Boney knelt by my side and gently dabbed my teardrops with his handkerchief. "There, now, mademoiselle," he said, placing the cloth in my hand. The letters "NB" were embroidered in gold upon it. "You may keep this, Betsy, as a token of our parting." He removed a small envelope from his jacket. "And this, *aussi*," he said, giving it to me.

The envelope contained four locks of the emperor's hair, tied with ribbons. He smiled mischievously. "One lock for Betsy," he said. "One for *mere et pere et les garçons*. And the emperor is so generous, he has even provided one for sister Jane."

I wiped my nose on my sleeve and managed a

small smile. "Are you sure you can afford to give away so much hair, Boney?"

"Very amusing, mademoiselle," he replied.

"Thank you," I said. "For the hair, I mean."

I stood up to leave. We looked at each other, knowing the end was now upon us. Briefly, I shut my eyes, straining to burn his features into my memory. And in the next instant, I felt that he was almost able to read my mind.

"You will forget me, mademoiselle," the emperor said with a sigh. "As my son will not remember his father."

"Never," I said, hugging him fiercely. "Never!"

He took my face in his hands and kissed me on both cheeks.

Briefly, I gripped the small, graceful hand that had led a thousand cavalry charges and dried my tears for me. Then I stepped back, turned slowly, and walked away.

He called out to me. "It is worth the time after all, mademoiselle," he said.

I turned around and looked at him quizzically. His voice was barely audible. His eyes were moist like a seal's.

"To make oneself loved," the emperor said.

I nodded. We understood each other. I walked

down the long, winding path to the sea, where my family and our ship awaited me.

I was twenty yards below the Longwood plateau when I suddenly remembered I had not actually said good-bye! The emperor was now gone from my sight, but I called out to him just the same. Would he—would he still be able to hear me?

"*Au revoir*, Boney!" I knew in English that meant only "until we meet again."

There was no reply. I supposed he had gone inside. Disappointed, I continued down the slope.

But then the emperor's voice floated down to me on the breeze, brightly, but without my optimism: "Good-bye, mademoiselle!"

At nightfall our ship in Jamestown Harbor raised anchor. I stood on the moonlit deck facing the island.

Good-bye, St. Helena, you palsied prison. Finally, I had the freedom I had sought for so long. But now that I did, I wasn't sure I wanted it. Without the emperor, I felt like I'd lost an arm—like the real Lord Admiral Nelson.

And yet freedom was the most important thing, was it not? Freedom! It had been Boney who had taught me to be truly free. Odd, I thought, to be schooled in liberty by a man who was a prisoner.

But then, who better to value its sweetness? With him to inspire me, I had done great things. He had literally taught me to fly.

In the end, I had failed. But was the emperor a failure for doing great things and falling short in the final days of his career? Did Waterloo erase all his successes? No, Boney was not a failure—and neither was I!

Still, I felt as the French people must. Their brave leader is gone and they wonder whether they can go on without him.

But Boney lost far more than I: his crown, empire, armies, his nation, his family, and his freedom. And yet he went on, did he not? With dignity and courage, in the face of all that. He had lost so much more than I was losing now.

If Boney could go on, then surely I must. And the emperor would expect no less of me.

It began to rain. I leaned over the ship's railing, watching the storm as we pulled away from shore. Lightning flashes ripped jaggedly across the sky. Off in the distance a dog howled—a lonely, horrible sound. I shuddered.

I felt a gentle hand on my shoulder.

"Don't be scared of the thunder, Betsy," Jane said. "I'm here."

I stared at her, surprised by her kindness. But for the next while she did not leave my side. We stood there at the rail, taking a long last look at the dark, black hump of St. Helena.

Jane held my hand. She was my sister, after all.

And far away, a pale yellow light hovered over Longwood.

It was three years later—some twenty years ago now as I write these words—on an unusually cold day in May 1821 when news reached me in London of the emperor's death.

Some say he was poisoned by his enemies. I know better. He died of a broken heart.

Epilogue

Nearly a year after that sad day in 1821, my husband, Mr. Abell, and I (yes, the unruly girl of my youth had blossomed into a rather appealing young woman, or so my husband claims; and would you believe it?—he is a distant relation of the execrable Ensign Carstairs!) were honeymooning in the north of France.

In a small town there we came upon a charming country inn and thought it would be a fine place to spend the night. While my husband unloaded our trunk from our carriage, I went inside to inquire about a room.

A man was bent over behind the front desk polishing his shoes. I stood before him, but he didn't notice me.

Weary, and getting a bit impatient to turn in for the night, I cleared my throat to catch his attention, but to no avail.

"Concierge!" I said, ringing the bell on his desk. *"Avez-vous une chambre, s'il vous plaît?"*

The man raised himself up slowly and looked at me. And to my astonishment, standing there before me was Emperor Napoleon Bonaparte!

My husband walked in dragging our trunk and found me dumbfounded, frozen like a statue in front of the desk. "Are—are you all right, darling?" my husband said. But my attention was wholly fixed elsewhere.

"It's me—me, Betsy!" I said to that old familiar face. "Betsy Balcombe!"

But the man behind the counter did not seem to recognize me. Tears came to my eyes—along with sorrowful realization. I trembled and extended my hand to him.

"It is a pleasure to meet you . . . ," I said, voice shaking with emotion, "Monsieur Roberaud."

Author's Note

Betsy Balcombe (later, Mrs. Abell) was a real girl who came to know and befriend Napoleon Bonaparte during the early years of his captivity on St. Helena. By some accounts, Betsy was fourteen when the emperor arrived on the island; others say she was thirteen. I chose to make her fourteen in my story so she could grow up more quickly.

In 1844 the real Betsy wrote an autobiography titled *Recollections of the Emperor Napoleon During the First Three Years of His Captivity in the Island of St. Helena, Including the time of his Residence at her Father's House, "Briars"* (London: John Murray). I have gone to enormous lengths to avoid reading this book as I feared it would be so charming that it might discourage me from having the temerity to attempt to tell Betsy's story in my own way.

While I encountered in the course of my reading only brief excerpts from Mrs. Abell's book, I have studied many of the accounts written by others who knew Napoleon—and Betsy—on St. Helena, including Dr. Barry O'Meara's book.[1] By all accounts, the emperor loathed Sir Hudson Lowe, his chief jailer. Some contend this antipathy was well earned.

---

1 Barry E. O'Meara, Esq., *Napoleon in Exile; Or, A Voice from St. Helena: The Opinions and Reflections of Napoleon on the Most Important Events in His Life and Government, in His Own Words,* 2 vols. (London: Peter Eckler, 1822).

Nearly all the characters in *Betsy and the Emperor*—including the rather silly Gourgaud, the gardener Toby, and the eccentric Huff—were based on real people, though Toby was actually Malayan, not Haitian. Even Tom Pipes, the Newfoundland dog, was a genuine resident of St. Helena—familiar to, though not owned by, the Balcombes. And Jonathan, the governor's tortoise, did indeed outlive both him and Napoleon and is still alive on St. Helena, at the ripe old age of about two hundred.

In my book I have quoted the real Napoleon Bonaparte more often than you would probably suppose. And a surprising number of the major and minor incidents in my story—for example, Betsy's turning the emperor's own sword against him, her "imprisonment" in the wine cellar, and her father's smuggling letters for Napoleon—really took place.

Napoleon was moved to Longwood on December 10, 1815. Governor Lowe arrived on St. Helena on April 16 of the following year. I reversed the order of these events so as to keep Betsy and her emperor together longer than might otherwise have been the case. And I telescoped the symptoms of Bonaparte's final illness so Betsy could witness more of it than she did in real life.

Betsy's attempts to help the emperor escape are my invention. At least, I think so—since, as I say, I have not read her book. But crazy old Huff did indeed believe it was his destiny to help the emperor escape from St. Helena. And the emperor's double, oberaud, existed. In fact, at least one author has suggested (somewhat ridiculously, in my opinion) that perhaps the man who died on St. Helena was Roberaud and not the real Napoleon.

The emperor passed from this world at 5:49 P.M. on May 5, 1821. As stated in my book, Betsy was not present for this event. The emperor's last words were: *"France, armée, tête de l'armée, Joséphine"* ("France, army, head of the army, Joséphine"). He was buried on St. Helena, and his body was removed from there for reburial in Paris nearly two decades later, where he was greeted by throngs of weeping Parisians, including some of his former soldiers.[2]

Present when Napoleon Bonaparte's body was exhumed on St. Helena were a number of his old comrades, including Gourgaud, the emperor's valet

2 Napoleon's tomb can be seen today at Les Invalides, a church in Paris. His remains are buried in six coffins, one inside the other: The innermost one is made of tinplate, the next of mahogany, then two of lead, another of ebony, and the outer coffin is oak, all inside a red porphyry (a type of rock) sarcophagus. Twelve pillars of victory surround it.

Marchand, Grand Marshal Bertrand, and Betsy's nemesis, Emmanuel de Las Cases ("*le petit* Las Cases").[3]

When the emperor's coffin was opened, an astonished Bertrand suddenly rushed toward the corpse. Napoleon's body was in a remarkable state of preservation. His fingernails and a beard stubble had grown after death, his skin was a healthy color, and his face and hands looked much as they had when his friends had known him. As Las Cases put it: "At the sight of what death had wrought—changes that were more like life than death in spite of the time that had elapsed—we were all suddenly overcome with feelings impossible to describe."[4]

Some historians theorize that the reason Napoleon's body was in such good condition after nineteen years in the ground was that he had been gradually poisoned by his enemies—Count Montholon or Governor Lowe perhaps?—using arsenic, an element with preservative qualities. Historians disagree about whether Napoleon was really murdered, but there is some evidence to support this. Modern tests by the FBI and Britain's Scotland Yard, among others, show traces of

3 Jean-Paul Kauffman, *The Black Room at Longwood*, trans. Patricia Marie Clancy (New York: Four Walls Eight Windows, 1999), p. 279.

4 Kauffman, p. 280.

arsenic in locks of Napoleon's hair that he gave friends as souvenirs. Whether the arsenic got into the emperor's system via enemies bent on murdering him or by natural causes (possible explanations for dangerously high levels of arsenic in his bloodstream might include eating shellfish, using hair tonic, taking medicine, or even exposure to toxins from the moldy green wallpaper at Longwood) is open to debate. Personally, I prefer Betsy's theory: The emperor died of a broken heart.

And now, if you will excuse me, perhaps I will finally get around to reading Betsy Balcombe Abell's autobiography. If she were still with us today, I think she might forgive me for writing this story in her name—for the purpose of exposing a whole new generation to Emperor Napoleon's softer side and the rough treatment he received at the hands of Sir Hudson Lowe.

Source Notes

Any quotes in this book attributed to Betsy, Napoleon, or members of his suite were either invented by me or taken directly from historical accounts: original sources, most of which were written by the emperor's staff who attended him on

St. Helena. Napoleon and his suite knew that his thoughts and words would be important to preserve for posterity, so they spent a good deal of time recording them on paper. Every day of his life on St. Helena is accounted for. In cases where I didn't have these original nineteenth-century sources myself, I had books quoting from them.

Examples of conversations from my book that (with only slight variation) really took place include Napoleon's "quizzing" Betsy about European capitals and boasting that he burned Moscow, as well as his warmly comforting and revealing comments when he spoke to her through the bars of her wine cellar "prison." Discovering the latter conversation was what first prompted me to want to tell Betsy's story.

Napoleon's own account of his triumphant return to Paris from his first exile in Elba is recounted in my book (almost) verbatim.

Gourgaud's whiny outburst at the dinner table—in which he complains of being a prisoner—and Napoleon's reply to it ("You are a brave man but amazingly childish," etc.) also really took place. It's also true that Gourgaud once saved the emperor's life (from "that Cossack at Brienne"), and never let him forget it.

In some cases I used in my story things Napoleon actually said at some point in his life (e.g., "The corpse of an enemy always smells sweet") but in a different context.

My research on Napoleon's actual personal habits and quirks also figured into the story. When angry, his left thigh muscle really did twitch due to an old war wound. He was indeed fond of licorice candy, had an amazingly retentive memory, was a bit of a prankster (the emperor loved mocking his "scary" image and once mussed up his hair and growled to frighten the Balcombe boys), and enjoyed playing games, like blindman's bluff and whist, and giving little gifts to children. The emperor also read plays aloud—very badly—and would become irritated when his staff members fell asleep while listening to him recite.

It was a bone of contention between Napoleon and his British captors that they refused to call him by his most recent official title, "Emperor." Perhaps it was one of the things that first intrigued Napoleon about Betsy—that she wasn't frightened of him but was also one of the few people on St. Helena, other than his staff, who paid him the respect of recognizing his proper title (Napoleon:

"And what am I, pray?" Betsy: "An emperor"). But she also called him "Boney," and he didn't seem to mind.

Geographical Notes

A map of St. Helena will reveal that if one travels (as Betsy does) from the Briars to Jamestown, one will not pass Plantation House along the way—at least, not without a very roundabout method of getting from here to there. I altered the two houses' positions relative to each other so that I could introduce my readers to Plantation House early in the story.

The island of St. Helena, one of the most remote places on earth, is still a dependency of Great Britain. Only 10.5 miles long by 6.5 miles wide, it is located in the South Atlantic Ocean at latitude 16°S, longitude 5°45' W; has no airport (though it may have one soon); and can be reached only by ship. St. Helenians were granted full British citizenship starting in 2002.

In my story Napoleon says to Admiral Cockburn that the "nearest land" to St. Helena is the continent of Africa, about 1,200 miles (over 1,900 kilometers) away. But in fact, the nearest land is Ascension Island—703 miles from St. Helena. Even if Napoleon knew of Ascension Island, it would have done him little good to escape to that tiny (35 square miles), isolated place, which is located in the South Atlantic Ocean, about halfway between South America and Africa. So this explains why, in my book, Napoleon says that Africa is the closest land to St. Helena.

The Code Napoleon and the National Anthem of France

THE CODE NAPOLEON

A full English translation of the French Civil Code ("Code Napoleon") drafted in 1801 and first published in 1804 can be found at http://www.napoleon series.org/reference/political/code.cfm. Napoleon considered the code to be his crowning achievement. It was really a reformation and consolidation of previous French civil laws, and Napoleon did not actually "write" the code—though he (and the commission of experts he organized, whose meetings he often attended) was unquestionably the driving force behind its creation and contributed ideas to it. The code—originally intended as a compact, one-volume guide to French law that any citizen could read and understand—is still the foundation of France's legal system today, and more than twenty nations have based their laws upon it.

THE NATIONAL ANTHEM OF FRANCE

"La Marseillaise," the national anthem of France—composed by army Captain Claude-Joseph Rouget de Lisle—began life in 1792 as "The Battle Song of the Army of the Rhine" during the French Revolution. A royalist, Rouget de Lisle would have been killed in the wave of public executions of supposed "enemies" of the state, the "Reign of Terror" that followed the overthrow of France's king, but his life was spared due to the success of his song.

"La Marseillaise" was declared a "national song" on Bastille Day in 1795. Ironically Napoleon himself, who had fought in support of the French Revolution, was not a huge fan of "La Marseillaise" and later banned it, possibly because he didn't want to encourage another revolution—against his own government. The ban continued under the Restoration, and "La Marseillaise" did not become the national anthem of France until 1879. As sung today, "La Marseillaise" is based on the "official" version adopted by the Ministry of War in 1887.

Excerpts from the lyrics to "La Marseillaise"

(with English translation next to the French verses) can be found at a Fordham University Web site: http://www.fordham.edu/halsall/mod/marseill.html.

Another translation of "La Marseillaise" can be found at the Web site of the Office of the French President (Presidence de la Republique) at http://www.elysee.fr/ang/instit/symb1_.htm.

Wendy's imagination never runs
away from her—it flies.

WENDY by Karen Wallace

An unforgettable novel inspired by the world of Peter Pan.